D0724759

# MILLIONS
## UPON
### MILLIONS

of years hence, when all of the ancient continents of Old Earth have come together to form the immensity of Gondwane, the Last Continent, in the Twilight of Time, there shall come a Savior sent by Galendil to wrestle with the Doom of the World: they shall call him Silvermane.

—OTH KANGMIR,
*The Book Imperishable*

Lin Carter

# The
# ENCHANTRESS
## of
# WORLD'S END

**DAW BOOKS, INC.**
DONALD A. WOLLHEIM, PUBLISHER

1301 Avenue of the Americas
New York, N. Y.        10019

For *Keith Laumer*,

a great guy, a grand writer,

and a Good friend.

FIRST PRINTING, MAY 1975

3 4 5 6 7 8 9

PRINTED IN U.S.A.

# CONTENTS

### Book One:
## THE ETHICAL TRIUMVIRS OF CHX

### Book Two: THE QUEEN OF RED MAGIC

### Book Three:
## THE GRANDFATHER OF ALL DRAGONS

### Book Four:
## THE MOBILE CITY OF KAN ZAR KAN

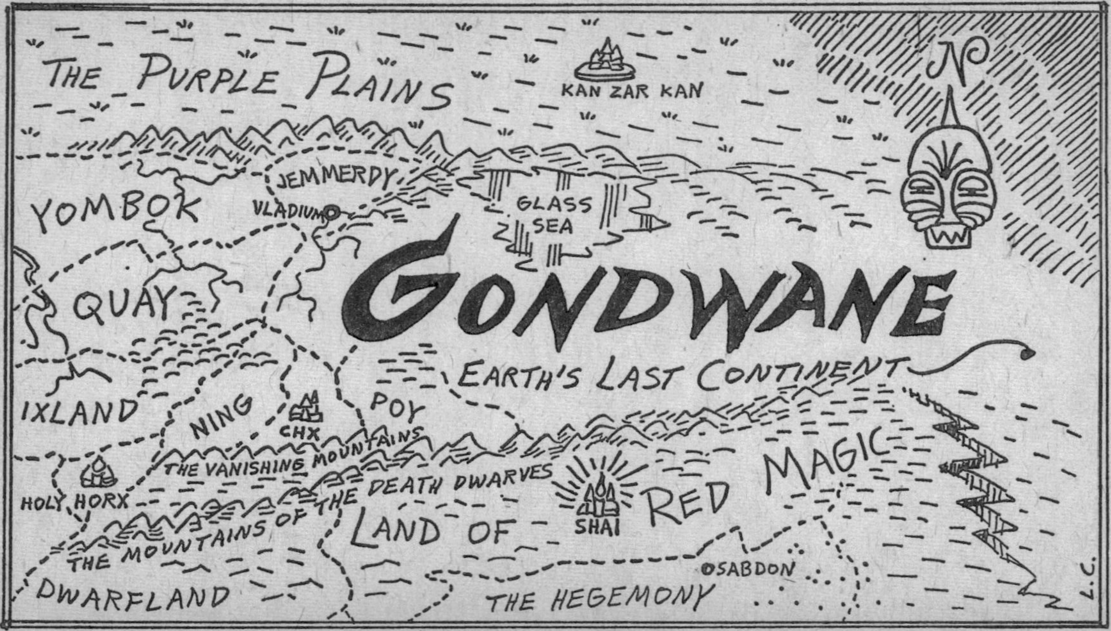

THE PURPLE PLAINS
KAN ZAR KAN
N
JEMMERDY
YOMBOK
VLADIUM
GLASS SEA
GONDWANE
EARTH'S LAST CONTINENT
QUAY
IXLAND
NING
CHX
POY
THE VANISHING MOUNTAINS
HOLY HORX
THE DEATH DWARVES
THE MOUNTAINS OF
LAND OF RED MAGIC
SHAI
DWARFLAND
THE HEGEMONY
SABDON
L.C.

# Book One

~~~~~~~~~~~~~~~~~~~~~~~~~~~~~~~~~~~~~~~~~

# *THE ETHICAL TRIUMVIRS OF CHX*

*The Scene:* Northern YamaYama-Land; The Wastes of Ning; The Free City of Chx; the Vanishing Mountains.

*The Characters:* An Illusionist, a Construct, a Girl Knight and the Bazonga; Chxian Townsfolk, Jailers and Triumvirs; Thirty-Two Death Dwarves.

# 1.
# THE SCARLET CITY

Through the skies of Gondwane the Great, Earth's last and mightiest continent, there floated an extraordinary vehicle. It bore the likeness of an ungainly Phoenix-shaped bird of dark bronze, with spread wings and peacock-tail, measuring some thirty feet from beak to tail-tip. For all that it should have weighed many tons, it soared as lightly as a wisp of cloud through the skies.

Behind the arched neck, and between the broad shoulders of the bronze bird-machine, a cockpit containing six seats was hollowed. The vehicle transported a remarkable foursome. In the "driver's seat," so to speak, reposed an elderly but vigorous man robed and gloved in glimmering silks, whose features were perpetually masked from sight behind a visor of lilac vapor. This personage was a powerful but friendly magician known as the Illusionist of Nerelon. For better or for worse, he regarded himself as the benign protector of these regions of north-central-eastern Gondwane—a position of responsibility he had, in a sense, inherited.

Seated beside him was a pert, long-legged, adolescent girl with a snub nose, a pretty, freckled face, sparkling green eyes under a mop of tousled red curls, full lips and a small, stubborn chin. She wore odd bits of steel armor—greaves, girdle, gorget, and the like. Her firm, pointed, tip-tilted breasts were also cupped in steel, and an abbreviated mail-skirt, which barely covered her rounded hips and left her tanned thighs deliciously bare, completed her curiously warlike costume. She was a girl knight from the distant kingdom of Jemmerdy where the women are the warriors and the men are all scholars, administrators, or aesthetes. Her name was Xarda.

Behind these two, uncomfortably squeezed into the second row of seats, towered a gigantic warrior. He had a grim-jawed, heavy-boned face, with fierce black eyes under scowling brows; the dark bronze of his naked hide was offset by his spectacular mane of glittering silver hair which poured over herculean shoulders and down his back. His bronzed torso, bulging with steely thews, was strapped into a war-harness of black leather. Between his shoulders an enchanted Silver Sword was scabbarded. He was a Construct, a synthetic superman created by the Time Gods for some unknown world-saving mission, and his name was Ganelon Silvermane.

I have referred to these persons as a remarkable foursome: the fourth individual of their company, possibly the most unique and curious of them all, was their bird vehicle itself, called the Bazonga. This animated aerial contraption housed a sentient crystalloid brain, connected by cunning electrodes to vision lenses, ear tympanies and a voice-box. It could thus see, hear, reason and speak; and, as its bronze body was rendered weightless by antigravitic yxium crystals, powered for flight by magnetic waves, it made the perfect companion of their travels.

At the time whereof I write, the four adventurers, having successfully terminated the menace of the Airmasters of Sky Island who had terrorized the Tigermen of Karjixia*, were enroute from the kingdom of the Tigermen to the realm of Jemmerdy in the east. The Illusionist had decided that the very least they could do to thank the girl knight for her share in their adventure was to assist her in returning home, before journeying themselves back to the magician's enchanted palace of Nerelon in the Crystal Mountains, south of the Voormish Desert. They had left the flying island

---

* As described in the first volume of the Gondwane Epic, a book entitled *The Warrior of World's End*, DAW, 1974.

early that morning, after ending the career of the tyran-
nical Elphod of the Airmasters; and, after a brief visit
to Xombol, the capital of the kingdom of the Tigermen,
where they had given Prince Vrowl the glad tidings
that his difficulties with the troublesome Sky Islanders
had been brought to a happy conclusion, they had flown
in the Bazonga bird all day across the regions of Northern YamaYamaLand.

Skirting the northerly borders of the dominions of
the Horxites, they had traversed the kingdom of Ixland
from west to east; and from thence along the northern
slopes of the Mountains of the Death Dwarves. At the
present time they were soaring high above a desolate
and barren region called Ning, which was inhabited
only by a few monastic settlements of Mind Worshippers. Late afternoon was upon them; the golden sun
of Old Earth declined in the west and the bleak landscape beneath their keel was drowned in purple
shadows.

"At this rate, my dear Bird, we shall be flying all
night, not to reach the capitol of Jemmerdy until some-
time tomorrow morning," remarked the Illusionist testily. "Had you not loitered along the way, we might
have been in Vladium by now, being wined and dined
in the hostelries of Xarda's homeland!"

"Oh dear me, I suppose you're right," their peculiar
vehicle clacked carelessly in her metallic tones. "But
the view was so interesting I simply did not have the
heart to speed my flight. Don't you find travel broaden-
ing, my dear?" the Bazonga asked the girl. "Personally,
after so many eons spent deep in the bosom of Gondwane, I find the experience *very* educational!"

The knightrix of Jemmerdy grinned at the quaint
Bazonga, as the ungainly bird artlessly prattled on. "By
my halidom, 'tis true," replied the Sirix Xarda wryly,
"but we mortals, composed of flesh and blood, unlike
yourself, require nutriment and repose. And, if we continue this interminable flight, my dear Bazonga, we are
not likely to enjoy either until mid-morn, when the
battlements of Vladium will hove into view."

"Perhaps we'd better land at some friendly city along the way, and secure lodgings," grumbled the Illusionist. "It has been so long since luncheon that my digestive processes are no longer on speaking terms with my mouth. Ganelon, you have the map, where are we, exactly?"

The bronze giant consulted the chart which he spread out on his lap. "Near the eastern edge of Ning, master," he replied in his deep voice. The Illusionist nodded briskly.

"Quite so. Well, we are not likely to find lodgings among the Ningevites; they are Mentalists, convinced in the non-existence of soul or spirit, worshipping the mind alone and cultivating its powers, which they augment and develop through the ceremonial imbibing of hallucinogenic drugs. A harsh, fanatic lot, with little inclination towards friendly hospitality. What lies beyond the bleak country of the Mind Worshippers?"

"The Free City of Chx," said Ganelon.

"Aye, that's true; I had forgotten. Chx. A small city-state to the north of Dwarfland, just over the Vanishing Mountains. Surely we can find some manner of hospice, inn or caravanserai in Chx . . ."

"Master—"

"As a matter of fact, it would be interesting to visit Chx," the Illusionist ruminated. "I have not been there in ages—in many years, that is. A colorful city, as I recall, with a local honey-wine most delectable—"

"But master—"

"—And a spiced meat pie you have to taste to be—"

"*Master—*"

—"lieve! Well, what *is* it, my boy?" the Illusionist snapped.

"Um. Nothing, really. But . . . remember how we got into trouble in Holy Horx on the last trip? And we were just going to stop there for the night . . ."

"Stuff and nonsense, Ganelon, you great lump! By the Purple Vortex, lad, have some faith in my powers, can't you? 'Tis not for naught that I am deemed preëminent among the magicians, wizards, sorcerers and thau-

maturgists of Northern YamaYamaLand! Dear me, all
we're going to do is take a room at an inn for the night,
and enjoy a hot meal and a comfortable bed for once,
after roughing it across the length and breadth of Gondwane all these weeks! *You* may require only the rudest
sustenance to revitalize your mighty frame, but these
old bones of mine need a bit of comfort from time
to time."

"Yes, master. I'm sorry, master," said Ganelon unhappily. "It's just that I don't want us to get into any
more trouble, like we did back in Horx."

"There is very little likelihood of that, my boy! The
Holy Horxites were religious maniacs who considered
everybody else in the world despicable heretics! But
Chx, as I seem to recall, is a decent, respectable, law-
abiding city, now under the benign government of the
Ethical Triumvirs—"

"And what are Ethical Triumvirs?" asked Xarda
curiously. "By my troth, magister, ne'er heard I of
such before."

"Well, ah, actually I'm not *quite* certain what the term
means," admitted the Illusionist. "But the people are
ethical and law-abiding in Chx, and not fanatical ad-
herents to any particular sect, like those madmen of
Horx. We shall spend a comfortable evening for once,
and simply stay out of trouble! Come, no more argu-
ments, now! I've decided on Chx, and that's all there is
to it. Ganelon, will you instruct the Bazonga on the
way thither . . ."

The giant warrior did as his master bade, and they
flew on into the east as the Sun sank in golden splendor
behind them. Ere long, the towers of the Scarlet City
of Chx rose before them and their ungainly flying vehicle brought them down to land in the bazaar of the
small metropolis.

And thus there was set into motion a sequence of
events which was to have exceedingly far-reaching con-
sequences for this portion of Old Earth in the Twilight
of Time.

# 2.

# *A QUIET EVENING IN CHX*

The travelers discovered the Scarlet City to be neat, clean and, as advertized, respectable.

The squares and bazaars of Chx were filled with a quiet, orderly populace who regarded the exotic Outlanders with curious but not unfriendly eyes. Ganelon and Xarda looked about them with interest: flowering trees lined the spacious boulevards, and these were neatly trimmed and clipped. The streets and sidewalks were recently swept and the doorsteps of the Chxian houses were freshly scrubbed, the houses themselves neatly painted. Everything within view was spotless, immaculate, in excellent repair. The Scarlet City was attractive, with its red towers and bright yellow houses, tinkling fountains and gay bazaars; the people themselves looked comfortable, happy, and well-fed.

The girl knight said in an undertone to Ganelon, "They certainly dress in an odd fashion!" The giant nodded silently, staring about him. While the Chxians were a pleasant-looking folk, they were robed and coifed with a somberness that he found quaint and odd. The men were clothed in sober hues of gray, brown, black or umber, with tight-fitting hose, knee-breeches, and buckled shoes. The women wore voluminous skirts in the same somber and joyless hues, and these skirts completely covered their lower limbs, while long-sleeved, high-necked bodices covered their upper bodies from neck to wrist. Even their hair was covered with stiff cloth, and their faces were devoid of cosmetics. Also, they wore no jewelry.

Even the children, who played quietly before the houses, were dressed in miniature replicas of the adult raiment. Accustomed to screeching, dirty-faced ragamuffins, the Illusionist found their quiet play a welcome relief and pooh-poohed the comments of his fellow adventurers.

"There is nothing here that need disturb us," he said with lazy good humor. "I gather that the Chxians are a highly moral, respectable people: what's wrong with that? So the women don't bare their bosoms, paint their lips, or bedizen themselves with gauds and bangles —what difference does it make? By the Ninth Plenum, you two worriers would find something to disturb you in the Paradisical Gardens themselves! Come along, now, and stop grexing!"

Ganelon exchanged a dubious glance with Xarda, then shrugged and fell in behind his master. But, like the girl knight, he found something oppressive in the extreme sobriety of Chx. Despite its bright colors, a gloomy pall of severe puritanism seemed to hang over the quiet streets, the freshly-painted houses, the orderly populace. And all about hung signs which proclaimed a variety of maxims. "STRONG DRINK, WEAK MORALS," one placard reminded. Another announced warningly, "FLIPPANCY IS FATAL," while a third glowered down upon them with the grim legend, "WHY SING AND DANCE WHILE DEATH IS NEAR?" Despite herself, the Sirix shivered slightly.

The Illusionist affably accosted the nearest of the Chxians who stood staring at the strangers curiously, if not disapprovingly.

"Tell me, my good man, is there an inn nearby where weary travelers can find a meal and lodgings for the night?" The Chxian nodded and replied, in neutral tones, that the nearest might be found on the south side of the bazaar square. Thanking him, the old magician led his companions to the threshold of the establishment which termed itself, in sober brown-painted letters, "The Hospice of the Twelve Cardinal Virtues."

"Come, come, you two, stop staring about apprehensively, and let us enter," he said testily.

Within they found a long, low-ceilinged room with tables and oaken benches neatly arranged before a cheerfully-crackling fire on a stone grate. The plaster walls were painted a solemn gray and the wooden rafters were neatly blackwashed; but the odors of meat turning on a sizzling spit were appetizing and the taproom, despite its lack of color or ornament, seemed snug and comfortable enough. A plump, sober-faced inn-keeper assigned them rooms for the night at a remarkably low fee and set dishes before them laden with hot meat, brown bread and fresh fruit, together with large mugs of a spiced drink which turned out to be an extremely mild ale whose alcoholic content was virtually nil. Tasting the meat, Ganelon found it a choice cut, but almost tasteless.

"Come, inn-keeper, have you no spices to enliven the flavor?" he grumbled. The placid-faced Chxian stared at him wide-eyed.

"Spices heat the blood and are a toxic moral influence," he said primly. "Solid, nourishing fare is the best."

"Aye, and this ale is excessively bland, by my troth," the girl knight grimaced after tasting it. The inn-keeper shrugged.

"Strong drink unhinges the reason and makes quarrelsome the temper," he replied, almost tonelessly, with the air of one repeating a maxim which frequent re-iteration had made all but meaningless. "You will find the beverage wholesome and filling, mistress, I am sure."

The Illusionist munched on the tough meat and took a swallow from his mug. He then glanced around at the somber room, whose only note of cheer came from the crackling fire. A number of soberly-dressed Chxians sat about conversing in a monotone, sipping their mugs, paying little or no attention to the Outlanders beyond a single, wide-eyed glance at Xarda's bare legs and Ganelon's skimpy loin-cloth.

"Your taproom seems remarkably quiet tonight," the Illusionist complained. "Can none of these fellows give us a merry tune on lute, pipe, or tambourine?"

The inn-keeper turned a cold eye on him. "Song and dance," he said, with a slight, fastidious shudder, "are cankers which devour the moral fiber of sinful men. We Chxians abhor the loose morals and ethical decay of foreign realms; sobriety, a clear head, and a quiet, respectable tongue are high among the virtues we celebrate. Your rooms are ready." And with that, and a slight, disapproving sniff, he turned on his heel and left them to their own devices.

"Hmm," the Illusionist grumped. "A dour lot, these Chxians! Well, let them be as glum and solemn as they please, so long as they let us be. Eat up children, drink deep, soft beds await our weary, toil-worn limbs!"

"Let's *hope* so," said Ganelon Silvermane gloomily.

Their three rooms were small and bare, devoid of furnishing, save for a narrow bed, a small table bearing a candle-stub in a pewter dish, and a chamberpot. The rooms were identical, even to the frowning placards on the walls which bore stern injunctions against licentious behavior such as "CONTINENCE LEADS TO QUIET SLUMBER" and "A CHASTE BED IS A RESTFUL BED." The beds themselves, mere cots, were hard and uncomfortable. Nevertheless, weary and well-fed, they were ready to retire.

Ganelon had accompanied the Bazonga to the stables at the rear of the hospice; finding the stalls too small to contain the huge creature, he had tethered her to a zooka-zooka tree in the courtyard. He came clumping up the stair to their adjoining rooms after the termination of this task with a wide grin on his habitually grim features.

"What's so funny, my boy?" inquired the magician.

"The inn-keeper," chuckled Ganelon. "I tied the

Bazonga bird to a tree in the courtyard and asked the inn-keeper if she would be safe there for the night on account of thieves. *Thieves!* I thought he would fall in a dead faint at the very suggestion. It appears that here in Chx thievery is about as rare as leprosy, and regarded with much the same degree of loathing!"

Chuckling, they bade each other good-night and turned to their respective rooms.

Night fell. The immense, cracked orb of the Falling Moon rose over the edges of Gondwane to flood the Supercontinent with silver light. And, with the coming of darkness, a most peculiar change came over the sober, respectable, Galendil-fearing people of Chx.

"Ganelon? *Hsst,* you great oaf; wake up!"

The giant blinked awake to find the supple, half-naked form of the Sirix Xarda bending over him, shaking his shoulder.

"What's happened—trouble?" he grunted, sitting up and reaching for the Silver Sword.

"*I'll* say," hissed the girl knight enigmatically. "Come take a look out of the window!"

The giant obediently clambered out of the cot and crossed the closet-sized room to peer out at the street below through glassy panes. What he saw from the window brought a rumble of astonishment to his lips.

By night, the streets of the Scarlet City were transformed into a fantastic carnival of revelry. Colored paper lanterns were strung across the streets, swinging gaily in the breezes. And through these streets, which by day were so exceptionally sober and respectable, surged a motley throng in gaudy festival garments. Most of the revellers carried flasks and bottles from which they drank heavily, the heady vapors of strong wines and brandies rising to the nostrils of Silvermane and Xarda. Musicians led the dancing throng with the patter of drums, the jingle-*thump*-jingle of gay tambourines and the tootle of pipes. Giggling bands of young children, naked except for flower-wreaths, fondled each other in doorways, while beneath every streetlight voluptuous women with unbound hair, their rounded limbs completely devoid of clothing, undulated to a hip-waggling dance.

"Great Gal-*en*-dil!" Silvermane gasped.

"You said it," the girl knight grinned. "Look down the alley there!" Ganelon followed her pointing finger to see a nude woman enthusiastically volunteering her services to five or six partially-unclothed men, in a complicated multi-embrace of considerable anatomical ingenuity. He gasped again, coloring faintly. "And there!" the girl pointed. A band of looters, having smashed in the windows of a shop, were busily emptying it of every last movable object. He stared out over the city, his amazement growing. Five masked bandits were quarreling over the plump purse of a lone quarry who stood helpless before their drawn knives while they squabbled. A bit further on a fat man sprawled, drunk and snoring, in a doorway while two stark naked, grubby-faced, grinning urchins relieved him of his purse, headgear, cloak and buskins. Further off, over the city, the sound of smashing windows came to them, the scuffle and thud of innumerable bar-room brawls, and a whiff of smoke from several burning buildings was evident. Snatches of wild carnival music, drunken song, and street-corner fights, drifted to them on the evening breeze.

"Has the entire city gone—*mad?*" asked Ganelon, puzzled. "Or have we?"

Xarda had no answer to his question.

# 3.
# THE MORNING
# AFTER

They went into the next room, where the Illusionist was, to find the old magician seated near the window peering out into the riotous streets with curiosity and just a touch of amusement.

"Master, have you—"

"*Sssh!* No chatter, my boy—and don't strike a light, either! We don't wish to attract undue attention, do we?" warned the magister. Xarda took one look at the figure of the old man, silhouetted against the pane, and clapped her hand over her mouth to restrain an attack of the giggles. For she had never before chanced to see the Illusionist accoutered for bed. He wore a loose nightshirt which exposed his skinny shanks, clothed in wrinkled hose, and his bony feet were shoved into a dilapidated pair of snuff-brown carpet slippers. He wore a long night-cap with a threadbare tassel at the end, she was amused to notice. But his veil of violet vapor was still in place. For a giddy moment, the girl knight wondered if he wore his mist-mask even in bed.

He seemed highly gratified by the spectacle of the streets below, and was peering out with an interest more clinical than voyeuristic.

"Heh, heh!" he chuckled dryly. "I was wondering about that. Delighted to see . . ."

"What?" asked Ganelon bewilderedly. "Wondering about what, master?"

"Well my boy, you know, when a people repress their natural human fleshly appetites to the degree the

20

Chxians have, such repressions cause a dangerous block-
age of the id which can, in time, lead to serious psy-
chosis. Puritanism is at one end of the spectrum of
human behavior, libertinism at the other. The wise man
selects a middle course—'Everything in moderation; but
a little of everything,' as wise old Ophion puts it. The
unwise, howsomever, hew to one extreme or the other,
to their error and eventual detriment."

Xarda observed the view from the window with
bright, interested eyes. Her quick wits had ascertained
the point of the Illusionist's rambling, philosophic discourse while Ganelon, of course, was still fumbling
along word by word.

"You mean," she started.

"Of course!" he snickered good-humoredly. "The
so-called Ethical Triumvirs, when they first imposed
these tight moral strictures on their people, must have
envisioned or guessed what would happen. So, with
commendable maturity of judgment, they imposed a
double law upon the Chxians. By day they are chaste,
sober, frugal, industrious, clean and moral to a fault.
But by *night*—"

"—By night, they are anything but!" giggled Xarda.

"Exactly, my dear! Doubtless, living by this double
standard engenders schizophrenia to some degree; but
that is far more wholesome than a blocked, congested,
sorely inflamed libido."

Ganelon, plodding dully behind, began to catch their
meaning.

"Do you mean to say," he demanded, still puzzled,
"that while by daylight the Chxians are moral, ethical,
scrupulously honest, law-abiding and sober—?"

"At night they turn into a bunch of thieving, mur-
dering sots and lechers," the Sirix chuckled. Ganelon
seemed shocked; the old magister, however, was fascinated. He began to pull his glimmering robes on
over his nightwear.

"Come, children, let's go down and enjoy the spectacle at first hand!"

"Are you sure we should?" said Ganelon, dubiously.

"Certainly. Why not? We are hardly likely to have our morals infected by the example of the Chxians, and they can do us no harm in their present state. Since we certainly won't get any sleep, what with all this clamor, we might as well get some fun out of it. Come —get some clothes on, and join me below!"

The taproom was transformed. From some hidden cellar, strong beverages had emerged and were being sold across the counter by the wainload. The long room was thronged, mostly by men in an advanced stage of inebriation, but there were more than a few women amongst them. None of these wore any clothes to speak of (unless a flower behind an ear, or a bit of jewelry here and there can be called "clothes"). They were either dancing with slow, wriggling, lascivious motions to the sultry atonal music of the pipes, or were busy being embraced, kissed and so on.

At least three fist-fights were in progress by the time Xarda, Ganelon and the Illusionist got downstairs, and one of these was developing into a splendid bar-room brawl. Ganelon was faintly shocked to see three or four civil monitors sitting at the bar, watching the miniature riot with expressions of sodden satisfaction on their faces. During the day, these same monitors in their stiff collars and uncomfortable tabards had been everywhere, suspiciously eyeing the populace, alert for the slightest signs of incontinence, indecency or inebriation. Now they were virtually wallowing in a den of sin, and seemed to be enjoying every minute of it!

The street outside was a shambles. Broken, looted shops gaped emptily; drunks slouched, snoozing in the doorways; thieves in black vizors with naked dirks lurked in every alley-mouth; men and women, reeling drunkenly in every conceivable state of disarray from gaudy carnival garb to total nakedness, staggered about giggling and embracing, dancing arm in arm.

A pungent cloud of mint-green vapor floated past from a band of sniggering, wobble-kneed loiterers. The Illusionist sniffed sharply, and laughed. "Crazy-weed! I didn't know they still grew it in these parts. No, my dear, thank you very much for the compliment, but I fear a man of my centuries is somewhat past such things!" This last comment was made to a heavily painted woman whose bodice was open to the navel, and who strolled about openly soliciting the attentions of unengaged males.

Ganelon, towering above the throng by head and shoulders, stared about him with an expression of gloomy disapproval of his glum features. *I fear I shall never understand True Men,* he thought to himself somberly.

Many a fight were in progress along the avenue, and some of the streets and squares they passed contained full-scale riots. Silvermane kept a wary eye out for trouble, and his hand was never far from a weapon, but nothing untoward happened to them during their tour of the streets of Chx. Any troublemakers still sober enough to walk could measure the heroic thews and towering height of the bronze giant, obviously, and decided to leave well enough alone.

"Tally-ho, there goes another riot!" laughed Xarda, as a growling mob went charging by, waving makeshift clubs in a belligerent manner. "And to think, earlier I was saying to myself that Chx was just about the dullest town I had ever visited!"

The Illusionist laughed. "Yes, my dear, quite a transformation, indeed! But *I* am wondering if this sort of thing goes on all night, or only for a pre-arranged period. Because if it *does* last until dawn, I am wondering what the poor Chxians do in order to get some sleep!"

Within another hour or so, the noise and bustle began to slacken sharply, answering the Illusionist's question for him. Those citizens determined on wife-stealing, infidelity, rape or more outre sexual encounters had already stolen away to some dark, cozy places; and the rest of the citizenry were either dead drunk, or had been bludgeoned into unconsciousness in this or that riot, fist-fight or bar-room brawl. Soon the city was peaceful again, and the travelers returned to their inn to snatch a few hours of slumber before daybreak.

What with being up half the night, it was only natural that they overslept by several hours the next day. Indeed, the sun was well up into the noonward skies by the time they roused themselves, washed, dressed, and came downstairs for some breakfast. The innkeeper, his gaudy carnival robes tucked away, looked stiff and solemn (and ever so slightly hung-over) in his modest daytime raiment as he served them a meager, spiceless but nourishing meal.

The Illusionist good-humoredly strove to engage the glum, puffy-eyed fellow in conversation concerning the riotous doings of the night, but the proprietor regarded them with eyes full of reproving severity at such flippant, suggestive talk and made a pointed reference regarding the civil monitors, which gave the old magician a clear hint to lay off. Obviously, what was done at night was never mentioned by day.

With one exception, however.

The Illusionist and Xarda were taking a brisk stroll in the square, prior to their departure, while Ganelon paid their bill, collected their gear and stowed it aboard the Bazonga. Suddenly a squad of stiffly-tabarded monitors approached, surrounding them.

"What seems to be the trouble, officer?" inquired the Illusionist, affably.

"It has been reported to headquarters that you and your companions committed numerous indiscretions during the nocturnal period, stranger," the leader of the squad replied. "I fear they are sufficiently serious to require you to accompany me to the constabulary. Come along quietly, now." And, so saying, he took the old magician firmly but politely by the arm.

" 'Indiscretions?' " repeated the Illusionist incredulously. "That's not true at all! We were remarkably discreet, considering the behavior of the local citizenry; why, we neither engaged in a brawl, nor got drunk, nor bothered any of the women! On the whole, we behaved with what I might term considerable decency and restraint!"

"Those are, to be precise, the very counts listed against you," said the officer sternly. "You are accused of nocturnal sobriety, continence, pacifism and public decency. Come along now; I don't want to have to clap you in chains."

Flustered, arguing volubly all the way, the magician was led off with Xarda in the direction of a large structure towards the center of the city.

# 4.

# UN-DISTURBERS OF
# THE PEACE

The central edifice into which the civil monitors
conducted the Illusionist of Nerelon and the girl knight
of Jemmerdy turned out to be the Administratium of
the city.

They were led into a domed rotunda where three
odd-looking officials sat at square wooden desks piled
high with papers. The first official, a lank, gloomy-
faced individual with thin, tight lips and an expression
on his face as if he sensed a singularly repugnant odor,
looked them up and down with sour disapproval
stamped on his long horsy face.

"Outlanders, I perceive!" he grumbled. "Always getting into trouble. Foreign riffraff! Ban the lot of ye one
of these days, if ye're not careful. *The count?*"

"Failure to disturb the peace during the nocturnal
period, my lord Nurdix," said the monitor, snapping to
attention.

The man at the second desk, a pudgy, sallow-skinned
little man with a bald, round head and squinting,
gelid eyes, snapped his fingers loudly.

"Be precise, fellow, when you address the Triumvir
Nurdix! The full list of particulars, *if* you please!"

"Sorry, my lord Glastro," said the officer, whereupon
he began to crisply rattle off a roster of crimes which
the Illusionist and his friends had *not* committed. Since
they had been guilty of no crimes whatsoever, the list
was extraordinarily lengthy. It began, in alphabetical
order, with Abandonment of Spouse or Offspring, Fail-

26

ure to Commit Same; Aberration, Sexual, Lack of; Abjuration of Sworn Oaths, Refusal to Do So; Abortion, Non-, and so on. The recital took forever, or anyway it seemed like forever. At about the time the monitor had got to Defenestration, Anti- or failure to throw anybody out of the window, a second squad entered the hall lugging the unconscious form of Ganelon Silvermane.

The third Triumvir, who had yet to be heard from, eyed the slumbering giant curiously. This third ruler, Petraphar by name, was a gray and mousy little wisp of a man with a soft, purring voice, veiled, elusive eyes and an annoying habit of constantly rubbing his hands together in a washing motion.

"Oh, my, and another one!" he lisped breathily. "That is correct—the bill of particulars *does* mention three of them. Goodness! Three nocturnal malefactors on the same day! A new record, I do believe. Tell me, captain, did the big man, ah, vigorously oppose his arrest?"

"You might say so, my lord," replied the captain through a mouthful of broken teeth. "A whiff of the sleep-gas laid him out, however; and the boys will be just fine, the Surgeon informs me, in a week or two at most."

"My, my! Well, just lay him down over there. Pray continue with the counts, lieutenant!"

The Illusionist cleared his throat. "If it please the court, I believe we can dispense with the full list of crimes which we unfortunately failed to commit. If your honors please, we are willing to concede ourselves guilty of, ahem, *not* committing every crime in, ah, the book. Except possibly for Ogling in the First Degree, which we did quite a bit of last night, heh heh!"

The Triumvirs were *not* amused. "Ogling is not a crime, merely a misdemeanor!" snapped glum Nurdix fiercely. "That will do, lieutenant; leave the document of complaint with the registrar on your way out. Smartly, now!"

The officer saluted and turned on his heel. The Illusionist stepped forward and began speaking amiably.

"If it please the court, I should like to point out that in no other country or city known to me, is the *failure* to commit a crime a culpable offence—"

"The customs in foreign realms have no bearing on the present case, sir," puffed fat Glastro imperturbably. Behind his veil of lilac vapor, the Illusionist blinked thoughtfully.

"Well, perhaps not, but your honors will realize that, as mere peaceful travelers, visitors to your fair city, just passing through, we had no fore-knowledge of the peculiarly Chxian criminal code—"

"Ignorance of the law is no excuse," whispered pallid little Petraphar, rubbing his hands together.

"But—surely, your honors can't hold us to blame for breaking a law so unheard-of as to be unexpected! How could we possibly have known—?"

*Law-abiding* travelers should make a point of inquiring into the local statutes upon the moment of entering a city," said Nurdix shortly. "Are we agreed, then, brothers?"

"Aye! Guilty as charged," said the others in a chorus.

"But—but—see here—you can't—" spluttered the Illusionist helplessly, as the monitors led him out of the room and down to the dungeons below the Administratium.

"Can't we, indeed?" smirked Glastro, in the ensuing silence. The other two Triumvirs laughed.

For a city as grim, colorless and dour as Chx—by day-time, at least—where even the inns provide few of the creature comforts, it would be folly to expect the jails to be comfortable. And, true to form, they were not. Furnished only with a wooden bench, a tin pot, and a pile of straw, they were harshly utilitarian.

"But at least it's a *clean* cell," said Xarda brightly, trying to put the best face on things. Grumbling and grexing, the old magician slumped in a corner and refused to be cheered up. Still unconscious from the sleep-inducing vapor, the bronze giant lay on the floor, snoring stertorously.

Seeing that she was not going to perk up the Illusionist with ease, the girl knight strolled about the stark little stone cubicle, eventually going over to the barred grille that served as a door. She tested the bars and found them firm; tried the lock and discovered it to be new, well-oiled and quite solid. Even Xarda could not help heaving a little dispirited sigh.

"I gather you are strangers to Chx?" said a male voice in a pleasing tenor. She looked up in surprise to find a tall, well-set-up young man standing at the door of the cell directly across the corridor. He was tanned and handsome in a well-bred way, with a finely-shaped head and clear-cut, if rather delicate, features. But his arms were admirably muscular and his shoulders strong-enough looking, which belied the slight delicacy she detected. His legs and torso were clothed in close fitting steel mesh, over which he wore the tattered remnants of a surcoat emblazoned with an heraldic emblem unfamiliar to her.

Catching her eye, he smiled pleasantly. Xarda frowned, then, with a slight shrug, decided to smile back.

"Strangers, by my halidom!" she swore bitterly. "Jailed for the non-commission of every crime in the book. And yourself, good sir?"

"Another un-disturber of the peace," he smiled. Then, making a courtly bow, he said: "Pray permit me to introduce myself, madam! Erigon of Valardus, at your service."

"I am the Sirix Xarda of Jemmerdy, and my companions in misfortune are a friendly magician called the Illusionist of Nerelon—for he seems to have no other name than that—and Ganelon Silvermane, the Hero of Uth, formerly of Zermish-city in the Realm of the Nine Hegemons."

"Good-day, then, to you all," said the young man amiably. "I fear your places of origin are unknown to me, perchance even as mine realm of Valardus be unknown to you . . ."

"Yes," the girl knight nodded, "I was about to ask you where Valardus was."

"Far to the north of here, beyond the Purple Plains, lieth my unhappy kingdom."

"Wherefore unhappy, sir?" asked Xarda, falling in with the young man's slightly antiquated mode of speech, which almost exactly suited her own.

"Alas, the fair glades and dells of gleaming Valardus now groan 'neath the tyrant's heel," he said, somewhat dramatically.

"Oh? What tyrant is that?" asked the knightrix.

"Zaar, as he calls himself. The Warlord, as his followers term him, in all their grim and martial myriads. 'Tis a mighty horde of savages, come wandering down from further north to ramp and roar through the tiny kingdoms of the lands Valardine . . . said Barbarians having over-run my realm, and tossed me forth upon the winds of chance, a homeless wanderer, who once upon a time could claim the very princely coronal—"

Xarda cleared her throat a bit impatiently; this old-fashioned roundabout way of talking was all very grand and stately in its way, but not ideally suited to the succint imparting of information. "Do you mean you're a Prince?" she demanded.

The chiseled features of the young man looked faintly pained at such curt inquiry, but he nodded. "Prince Erigòn of Valardus," he admitted. "Or such at least I was when Good King Vergus held the throne! My hereditary throne!" She looked blank. "My late father," he added. "Oh," she said.

Along towards noon, a jailer came shuffling down the corridor to ladle a greasy and unappetizing stew into tin dishes from a common bucket. He eyed the knightrix primly, thin lips clamped shut in an expression of sour disapproval, failing to reply to several questions she asked of him. Among these were, "What are they going to do to us, and When?"

By this time, the old magician had recovered much of his good-humor and tackled the cold stew with a degree of zest the girl knight found repulsive and annoying. She had noticed, on similar occasions how the Illusionist seemed to virtually thrive on hardships, perils and adventures. He had once explained that after a long, fairly dull and uneventful career of magicianhood, a few dangers, imprisonments and excitements like these were a welcome change from unrelenting safety and security.

She was no limp-hearted weakling, was Xarda of Jemmerdy; but after the colorful, unsettling events of the last few weeks, she could happily have suffered through a bit of that same safety and security.

By this time, Ganelon had recovered from the sleep-inducing vapor, and gloomily prowled the narrow cell, testing the bars of the door until they squealed and squeaked. The giant did not enjoy captivity, and such were his incredible thews that the girl knight wondered if they should have to suffer very long. Indeed, next to Silvermane, the door of steely bars looked somewhat fragile and flimsy.

"Relax, my boy," advised the old magician, chewing with relish on the greasy stew. "Even if you did rip the door off its hinges, which perhaps you could, we should still face an entire city filled with enemies before reaching the outside world. Relax, and keep calm."

"I'll try, master," said Ganelon. "But I keep worrying about the poor Bazonga, and what these crazy people may be doing to her . . ."

"The dear Bird can take care of herself, as you will doubtless learn," said the magician cheerfully. "No doubt she is still floating in the courtyard of the hospice, obediently tethered to her tree, amusing herself by singing little songs. I doubt if the so-called Ethical Triumvirs have any notion the vehicle is animate, much less sentient. *Do* stop that pacing to and fro, my boy! Sit down and have some stew. Save your strength, for the time when we shall need it."

"And when will that be?" asked Xarda with a sigh.

The Illusionist winked, although she couldn't see the wink, with his vapor veil covering his features.

"When we make our escape," he said comfortably.

"And when will *that* be?" she repeated the question.

"Soon enough," he said, with a smugness she found rather irritating. It was annoying to share adventures with people who refused to take danger seriously, she thought to herself. But there was no use complaining about it. Wiping his lips and taking a swig of fresh water from the pail, the Illusionist settled back on the bench, folded his hands in his lap, and seemed to doze.

How could anybody take a nap at a time like this? Xarda swore under her breath, and turned back to the door to start another conversation with the pleasant young prince across the corridor.

# 5.
# OF THE XIMCHAK HORDE

During the rest of that afternoon, Xarda and Prince Erigon got better acquainted, while the old magister napped and Ganelon moped and sulked gloomily to himself.

In a rather hazy fashion, Xarda was familiar with the local geography of this part of the Gondwane supercontinent. She knew the Free City of Chx was directly north of Dwarf-Land, across the Vanishing Mountains, whatever they were; and that north of Chx were many little dukedoms, princedoms, city-states and kingdoms, with Jemmerdy itself northeast of Quay. And she knew that to the north of Jemmerdy and the Glass Lake, there stretched an interminable region of flatland called the Purple Plain, whereon the ferocious Indigon herds wandered and the Moving Cities were occasionally seen. But whatever realms might, or might not, lie north of the Purple Plain were thoroughly unknown to her.

This slight geographical ignorance in the education of the Jemmerdine girl is quite understandable, when you pause to consider the true immensity of Gondwane. In the seven hundred million years between our own Twentieth Century and the Eon of the Falling Moon, the theory of the continental drift was more than proven scientifically accurate. The continents did indeed form one vast land mass (called Pangaea) in Time's Dawn; tidal forces did cause the breakup of the primal supercontinent and set the various fragments into a slow drifting apart. But, after enormous ages of time, they

33

came together again on the opposite side of the globe, until now, in the Twilight of Time, a second Supercontinent had been formed, which comprised the total land surface of the planet.

The continent of Gondwane, therefore, was vast. Unthinkably vast! Picture Africa, Antarctica, Australia and the Americas, to say nothing of all the various islands, from Greenland on down to Wak (which is the smallest island in the world), all piled together in one interminable expanse of dry land, then you will have some notion of the true extent of Gondwane the Great.

The Supercontinent measured fully sixty million square miles from shore to shore. And sixty million is rather a lot of square miles, you will agree. Room enough on Gondwane for no fewer than one hundred and thirty-seven thousand kingdoms, empires, citystates, federations, theocracies, tyrannies, conglomerates, unions, principates, democracies, republics, plutocracies, realms, nations and countries. So many, in fact, that no one person—not even a professional geographer—could claim familiarity with them all. Which may help to explain why Xarda of Jemmerdy did not know where the kingdom of Valardus was.

Or where it had been, that is. For, having been ground into the dust by the Ximchak Horde, it could no longer be presumed to exist. Such, at least, was the belief of Prince Erigon, or the former Prince Erigon, since homeless exiles enjoy only slender claims to monarchial titles.

The old magician was quite interested to hear some firsthand observations concerning the Ximchak Barbarians, from an eye-witness to their horrendous depredations. Quite some time ago he had confided to Ganelon that they comprised, with the Airmasters of Sky Island and the mysterious Queen of Red Magic, one of the three greatest dangers to the peace and security of this part of Gondwane. Now he eagerly queried the pleasant Prince on their strength, number, equipment, temper, customs, religion and military prowess.

"As to how great their numbers may be, I have no precise knowledge, magister," Erigon replied. "For I was absent from Valardus when they descended upon the kingdom; my royal father, King Vergus, had dispatched me upon a mission of desperate urgency to the neighboring realms about, hoping to solicit forces to make a concerted stand against our common enemy. Alas, the Ximchak patrols were out in force, and cut me off from the pass through the mountains. I was forced to seek a rather wandering and circuitous route which I followed in a southerly direction. Completely losing my way, I wandered from city to city and realm to realm, eventually finding myself here in this abominable city of Chx. Like yourselves, my failure to partake in the nocturnal criminalities resulted in mine imprisonment. I am now so far away from my unhappy natal land that I despair of ever finding my way back . . . not that there is likely to be anything left of fair Valardus for me to return home to!"

Ganelon cleared his throat fretfully.

"Master, why are we sitting here talking? Shouldn't we be attempting to escape, before these people execute us for our non-existing crimes?"

"All in good time, my boy, all in good time," chirped the Illusionist in his cheerful way.

"But, magister, the boy doth have a point," argued Xarda firmly. "Whatever *are* we waiting for—surely, with your mastery of the Arts Magical, 'twould be an easy matter to unhinge yon door and dispeople the entire building—"

The Illusionist clucked her into silence.

"You children, with your constant fretting over time lost, spent or wasted!" he sighed. "As if an hour or two, or even three, mattered when measured against a lifetime! Had I harkened to your urgings, I would have resisted arrest or trial or imprisonment with my small skill—to our considerable detriment, for then we should not have made the acquaintance of Prince Erigon, here!"

"Yes, 'tis true, of course, but—!"

"But nothing, my dear child. We shall be set free when it pleases the good Galendil to free us, and not before," said the old magician, testily. "For one thing, my dear, has it occurred to you that as soon as night falls, Chx will return to her normal routine of murder, arson, burglary, rapine, and other assorted malfeasances? What better occasion for jail-break, than during that period of the night when such is no longer to be considered a crime?"

The girl knight blinked as if thunderstruck, then burst out laughing.

"Of course! As soon as night falls, the guards will be withdrawn, so as to partake of the assorted skullduggeries in which each Chxian must, by law, indulge. Forgive me for doubting you, magister! I fear that I had not fully thought through the implications of Chx's dual legal system . . ."

"Quite all right, my dear; that's what older and wiser heads are for. Now, my dear Prince, to return to our most interesting discussion of the Ximchak savages . . . I believe it was your opinion that they descended through the mountain countries, approaching Valardus from the north. Could it not, perchance, have been from the northwest? My own sources of information, you see, suggest a northwesterly course for the Horde, following their destruction last year of the Thirty Cities of the Gompish Regime . . ."

The sun of afternoon declined into the west. However swift the judicial processes of the Chxians might be, the final sentencing certainly seemed a drawn-out and lengthy process. Prince Erigon, they learned, had been condemned to the dungeons beneath the Administratium some four or five days before, on charges of being an un-disturber of the peace. And he still awaited his sentencing.

"Sometimes it is to be chained to labor in the water mines," he told them. "Other offenders are condemned to penal servitude repairing the aqueduct system. A former cell-mate of mine, an Ixlander, I believe, who acted as a travelling salesman in warlockry with a line of talismans and sigils, ended up serving his term as a sewer-cleanser. An unpleasant task, surely, and a stenchful one, to boot!"

Before sundown, the prisoners were removed from their common cell and were escorted by a squadron of monitors so numerous and stoutly armed for resistance to be futile, if not sanguinary, to private cells higher up in the monstrous edifice. Ganelon did not care to be separated from his dear friends, but no choice in jail accommodations was offered to him, and his master cheerfully bade him be of good spirits and not to fret. Therefore he complied with docility to the new arrangement, and found himself in a cell somewhat smaller even than before, whose door was a solid panel of adamant. The one factor of comfort in his new quarters was that his cell had a window, albeit one heavily barred, which gave forth on a wide prospect of the rooftops and spires of Chx. From this orifice he peered gloomily out upon the westering sun as it sank to its conflagration in the hills.

He wondered where Xarda and the old magician were housed, and why their cells had been switched, and how long would it be before the Illusionist came to free him from his durance? And whatever had possessed them to seek accommodations for the night in this mad metropolis in the first place.

After a time he dozed.

"YOO-HOO! Is that you, dear boy?" a familiar, if unexpected, voice hailed him through the mists of sleep. For a moment, convinced that he dreamed, Ganelon kept his eyes closed. But then a *whump* shook the walls of his cell with staggering impact, bringing down flakes of plaster from the ceiling in a gritty shower.

He opened his eyes and jumped up to see a beaked bronze head peering at him with brightly inquisitive eye-lenses through the bars of the window. It was the Bazonga bird!

"Wh-whatever are *you* doing here?" he asked, inanely.

The Bird cocked a disapproving eye at him and sniffed in a hurt manner. "Tush! You certainly don't seem glad to see me," she complained.

"Well, of course I'm glad to see you; but how . . . I mean, why . . ."

"You folks went away and left me all alone," the Bird said accusingly. "I sang little songs to myself, watched the stars go wheeling overhead and counted the leaves on the zooka-zooka tree to which you tied me. Morning came, then mid-morn, then fore-noon, then noon itself. Well, my goodness, I got to feeling lonely! So I decided to come looking for you."

"But however did you find me? Behind all these stone walls, I mean?" The Bird tartly reminded him of her ability to sense the radiations of an individual human aura, and to tell one auric spectrum from another, which was the method by which the Illusionist and she had found him and Xarda in the jungles of Karjixia, after their escape from the Air Mines on an earlier adventure.

"Now stand back, do," she carolled. Without further ado, the animate vehicle rammed her bronze beak into the outer wall of his cell in an effort to free him.

# 6.

# *FLIGHT FROM CHX*

The talking vessel was built of solid bronze and measured some thirty feet, from her parrot-beak to the tip of her peacock-tail. When a flying battering-ram of that size, weight and mass drives itself against a wall of mortared stone, well, *something* has got to give. In this case, it was the wall.

Bits of stone and chips of mortar sprayed the room, rattling off the walls and floor-tiles. Ganelon shielded his eyes with his burly fore-arm, and as soon as the whirling cloud of stinging rock-dust cleared away, he blinked through watering eyes to see a fairly man-sized hole punched directly through the outer wall of his cell. The Bazonga's battering thrust had carried away the lower portion of the wall in which the window was built. Now the bars waggled uselessly in empty air, and even as he watched, one of them clanked to the gravel-strewn floor.

"Come along, there's a dear," the Bird sang carelessly. Wobbling on her magnetic waves, she maneuvered herself about in such a manner that her cockpit now yawned temptingly just beyond the hole in the wall. Ganelon climbed through the opening and stood there indecisively for a moment, not certain whether to go or to stay.

"Come along, smartly now, there's a good boy!" snapped the Bazonga. "If you think it's *easy* holding a steady keel in such a position, let me inform you otherwise!"

"Yes, but—what about master, and Xarda? Shouldn't

we rescue them, too, so we can all leave together?" asked Ganelon bewilderedly.

The Bird wiggled her wing-tips impatiently.

"Time enough for that later," she said crossly. "I want to carry you to safety first. This is *my* rescue, and I am in charge! As soon as I get you over the border, I'll come whizzing back for the others. Serve that old geezer right, to make him wait a bit and stew in his own juices! Always tying me up to trees or chimneys, and leaving me behind while the rest of you go zipping off to have adventures together, with never a thought for the poor old faithful Bazonga, your tireless steed! Come, child, get into my cockpit and let's be off—"

"Well . . . all right, then . . . I guess you know what you're doing," said Silvermane a bit dubiously. He stepped into the swaying cockpit of the peculiar craft and settled down in the first seat. The bird-vessel thrust herself clear of the wall with a flick of her magnetic waves, then curved sharply about and sped off in a southerly direction, bound for the borders of Chx.

Night had fallen by now, and the streets were full of carousing mobs happily assaulting each other, looting shops and getting drunk. Nobody seemed to pay the slightest attention to the winged bronze bird as she soared over the rooftops and hurtled gaily into the south. So rapid was her flight that in less time than it takes me to tell, the scarlet walls of Chx dwindled in her wake. The landscape, neat, trim checkerboard of cultivated farmland, sped by beneath her keel. Ahead yawned vast empty pits which were sometimes occupied, and sometimes not, by the Vanishing Mountains.

"I find it simply amazing, the facility you poor humans have for constantly getting into trouble," groused the Bazonga bird as she traversed the farmlands like an immense arrow loosed from some colossal bow. "However do you manage to do it? I no sooner get tied to a tree or whatever, then you are off getting jailed for one reason or another. The last time this happened, if I recall correctly, you and that nice girl were sold into slavery . . ."

"Yes, that was in Horx," said Ganelon. "I don't understand it either, Bird, to be frank. Ever since father and mother found me wandering about in the Blue Rain, it's been one predicament after another . . ."

The vacant roots of the Vanishing Mountains were beneath them now. Ahead stretched a dark, grim landscape of tumbled stone and sterile sand, with the mighty ramparts of the Mountains of Dwarfland to the south, marching from horizon to horizon. The sight reminded Ganelon that the Death Dwarves were their enemies, and on at least one occasion, they had sought to capture them. There was that time when they had been flying across the Voormish Desert, bound for Karjixia, the Kingdom of the Tigermen, when the little green abominations had sought to ensnare them in a monstrous metallic net stretched directly in their path between the twin peaks of Mount Luz.

"Why are we flying in this direction?" he asked uneasily. "You're going south, and we want to travel north, towards Jemmerdy."

"Because the nearest border is south of Chx, that's why," replied the Bird tartly. "That nice inn-keeper back at the hospice told me. The sun was down by then, you see, and he was more than delighted to aid and abet a jail-break." She giggled at the odd ways of humans.

Just beyond the empty row of enormous pits, the Bazonga floated down to the ground and let Ganelon jump out.

"You stay right here, now," she said severely. "Don't go wandering off and get into any more trouble, mind! I'll just be a little while, finding your master and that nice girl—"

"And Prince Erigon, too," said Ganelon. "I'm sure master will want to rescue him, as well."

"Quite right, whomever you mean," the Bird said

in her careless fashion. She rose up from the ground and spun about to go back in the same direction from which she had just flown.

"And don't forget my sword!" Ganelon yelled as she drifted aloft. "I'm sure master will be able to find it somewhere in the building, and I'd be lost without it."

"Yes, yes, I shan't forget! Now, you be a good boy, mind, and don't go wandering away; I'll expect to find you right here when I return!"

Ganelon nodded and waved goodbye. The ungainly vehicle shot off to the north, towards Chx, and he stood watching her for a moment. The immense glowing orb of the Falling Moon had risen up over the world by this time, flooding the landscape with brilliant silvery luminance. By the moonlight, the terrain about him looked even more barren and sterile than it had from above. He repressed a slight shiver which came over him for some reason. Then he sat down on the stone slab to patiently await the return of the vehicle.

The Vanishing Mountains, which form the southerly borders between the country of Chx and the Dominion of the Death Dwarves, are a phenomenon unique to Gondwane in the current Eon. Nature, in a state of flux, persists in devising new, novel forms of matter and kinds of life (such as the Dwarves themselves). The prevailing theory by which the Gondwanish savants explain such curiosities, as these off-again-on-again mountains which flicker back and forth between existence and non-existence, is that the atoms whereof the rocky barrier is composed consist half of normal electrons and protons, and half of contraterrone particles, with a single phi-meson on the dividing line. The phi-meson, of course, is a particle of dubious reality, whose genuineness is a matter of statistical probability. Part of the time the meson really exists, and thus so do the Mountains; the rest of the time the finicky little particle simply isn't there at all, and neither are the Mountains.

The appearance and disappearance of the peculiar

mountain-range is, after all, a matter of little or no importance to anybody in particular. The cliffy heights are not inhabited by anything more lively than a few scruffy lichens and a small colony of disagreeable land-crustaceans, or mountain-dwelling lobsters, who formerly were denizens of the sea. That was a couple of dozen thousand years ago, when the Inland Sea of Voorm occupied most of the barrens about this part of Gondwane. Then the Vanishing Mountains were forced skywards by geological forces, when the crust of Old Earth buckled hereabouts, and the sea receded and finally drained away into the bowels of the planet. Suddenly finding themselves marooned high and dry on the mountain-peaks, the local variety of lobster would doubtless have died out, had it not been for a sympatheic magician in the neighborhood who cast an enchantment over them, turning them into mountain-dwellers.

The magician in question, an affable personage called Ulph the Unpredictable, had an innate fondness for marine life which was quite understandable, when you pause to consider his lineage (his mother, that is, was one of the Mer-folk).

Even a land-dwelling lobster, by now inured to sudden changes in habitat, finds it difficult to adjust to blinking in and out of Reality At the period whereof I write, the lobster-colony had been ruminating for some generations a planned migration to the lowlands, away from the Vanishing Mountains. But this is neither here nor there—like the Mountains themselves

I mention all of this merely to point out the unpredictability of the existence of the Mountains

They were not there when the Bazonga flew Ganelon to safety; on her return flight, however, the poor creature was less fortunate.

Suddenly, a gigantic wall of rock zoomed up right in front of her nose, so to speak. With a startled squawk, the ungainly animated contraption strove to put on the brakes, but slammed into the rocky wall nonetheless.

Solid bronze is, of course, a tough and durable metal —far less easily broken than steel, for example. Ferrous metals possess a lamentably frangible crystalline structure which permits them to fracture with surprising ease. Hence the bronze bird-vessel was not particularly damaged, even by a head-on collision with a mountain-range.

But her crystalloid brain was somewhat less durable. The impact seemed to stun the poor Bazonga. Her eye-lenses dulling, her beak-jaws wobbling open, she floated back from the impact and drifted idly on the night-breezes, which impelled her to and fro.

From their clefts in the rocky wall, the mountain-dwelling lobsters surveyed the ungainly creature with stalked eyes a-glare. This was the last straw, certainly! If thirty-foot metallic monstrosities were going to be banging into their mountains from now on, surely it was time to decamp for the comfort and relative security of the lowlands! Packing their supplies of edibles, and rounding up the young ones, the heartily offended crustaceans began to migrate in unison, crawling down the slopes of the Vanishing Mountains and paying no further mind to the vacant-eyed Bazonga as she drifted lifelessly on the wind.

# 7.

# ESCAPE TO JEOPARDY

From his narrow cell, which was on the interior of the Administratium and, windowless, the Illusionist of Nerelon had no way to judge the moment of nightfall, save for the peculiar behavior of the monitors set to patrol the dungeons.

Promptly at the hour of Moonrise, one of the hard-faced monitors threw down his yarmak, plucked out a bit of chalk from a pocket in his kilt, and began to scrawl something on the wall. Peering interestedly through the bars, the Illusionist could just make out the graffiti. It read:

### GLASTRO, NURDIX AND PETRAPHAR ARE A BUNCH OF OLD MEANIES!

His commentary on the rulership of Chx completed, the monitor slunk down the hall to see if he couldn't rob the off-duty guards, asleep in the barracks.

Grinning to himself, the Illusionist rose to his feet, yawned and stretched lazily, and hurled a minor enchantment at the door of his cell, whose strong metal bars promptly turned to rubber. Stepping out into the corridor, the Illusionist began searching about for his friends. Xarda he discovered, pacing her cell irritably. The girl knight of Jemmerdy was much relieved when the robed and mist-masked magister popped into sight, and even more relieved when the bars of the cell-door wilted like yesterday's asparagus.

Ganelon they could not find at all, but Prince Erigon, still locked in the subterranean dungeon, was easily found and freed. Using the Third Eye of occult vision, which functions only on the next highest plane of the Plenum, which is called the Astral, it was simple for the old magician to locate the cells of his companions. Auric spectra are clearly visible on the Astral level, and stone walls happen to be invisible on that plane.

"I can't understand what could have happened to Ganelon," the Illusionist said fretfully. "I've searched the entire area of space occupied, on the Physical plane, by the Administratium and his aura is nowhere to be seen."

"Could he possibly have escaped, all by himself?" inquired the Sirix, a trifle anxiously.

The magician shrugged. "It's possible, I suppose. The dear boy possesses remarkable strength, and the Time Gods outfitted him with more than a few extraordinary powers which are seldom the possession of ordinary humans. Most of these super-abilities remain mere potentials, as yet, but under stress or duress, there is simply no guessing what the Great Lump might not be able to do."

"Well, what are *we* to do? Just go off and leave him?" she demanded. The magician shrugged helplessly.

"I don't know what else there *is* to do!" he confessed. "This is obviously our best opportunity to escape from our captivity and gain the outside world unmolested and unpursued. Once we are free, and have found a place of relative safety, I should be able to ascertain the lad's whereabouts by means of sortilege or divination. Come, then; let us be off."

Xarda chewed her lip unhappily. Then, hefting the huge length of the Silver Sword, she said, miserably: "I suppose you are right. At any rate, we have found his magic weapon for him . . ."

Prince Erigon cleared his throat, a small, polite sound.

"I dislike abandoning a comrade as heartily as do you, for all that my acquaintance with the fellow has been very much briefer, but permit me to suggest that, while we stand here discussing the question, trouble approaches." He gestured; down the hall a crew of rowdies approached, lustily swigging from small jugs of brandy, and reciting obscene limericks at the top of their lungs. From their soiled and disarranged tabards, it was obvious that the quarrelsome rabble, during the daylight hours, doubled as civic monitors.

Due to the regular night-time crime wave, everybody that should ordinarily have been on duty at the Administratium was off robbing stores, mugging passers-by, tying tin cans to the tails of domestic pets, or committing a malfeasance. The Illusionist, the knightrix, and Prince Erigon of Valardus found it quite easy to escape from the central edifice of the city, with a little help from one of the magician's invisibility spells.

They returned to the Hospice of the Twelve Cardinal Virtues to find the taproom a seething mass of drunken, struggling men; eluding the several thieves, assassins, burglars and footpads who lurked in the shadows, they went around to the back. They entered the courtyard where they had left their peculiar aerial vehicle, tethered by a mooring-line to one of the tall, flowering zooka-zooka trees.

The tether was still there. So was the tree. But as for the Bazonga, it was obvious that the Bird had flown.

"What do we do *now*, prithee?" demanded the knightrix of Jemmerdy in a fine temper.

Unfortunately, for once the Illusionist had no adequate reply to make.

After a while, Ganelon was weary of sitting on the stone slab and stood up, looking around him. Turning to cast a glance behind him, he blinked with surprise to discover a gigantic range of mountains blocking the landscape to the south. The mountains had not been there when he and the bird vessel had flown hither; these must be the Vanishing Mountains whereof he had heard so much. He eyed the beetling ramparts with interest: considering they were made of stuff which was only half real, at best, they certainly *looked* solid and substantial to the untutored eye.

He was still admiring the mountains by moonlight when the Death Dwarves fell upon him.

There were thirty-two of the little green devils, although of course he swiftly became too busy to bother with counting them. He had never before seen one of the odd little monsters up close, and was not particularly happy to discover they were every bit as ugly, as formidable, and as vicious as common rumor made them out to be.

Their average height was somewhere between two-and-a-half and three feet, which meant that they hardly reached above Ganelon's kneecap. They were colored a vile, poisonous green, covered with lumps like warts only about the size of doorknobs. Their tremendous breadth of shoulders and thick, massively-thewed arms and barrel chests reminded him of the Indigons he had battled on the Plains of Uth.

Bald and hairless, with bullet heads, they had heavy prognathous jaws and long, lipless, gash-like mouths that made them look rather froggy. Froglike, too, were their ugly, goggling eyes which glistened in the moonlight like puddles of spilt ink.

They didn't wear any clothing to speak of, just odd bits, scraps and pieces of iron armor; but they bristled with weapons. Among these were flint-knives, stone axes, clubs roughly carven from petrified wood, and long spears made from slender stony stalactites, with obsidian blades for points.

They had no ears, and conversed amongst themselves in clicks, squeaks and hissings. They also had no genitals, just bare tough flesh between their crooked little bowlegs, which terminated in ugly, four-toed feet. They emitted a vile medicinal stench, like iodine. The insides of their mouths were black. And they had fat white tongues, like plump worms.

They had obviously been creeping up behind him for

some time, taking advantage of the bewildering moonlight to crawl and scuttle among the tilted stone slabs, waddling splay-footedly from inky shadow to inky shadow. Now that they were discovered, this furtive slinking ended abruptly, and they hurled themselves at him with dizzying speed, bouncing across the slabs like so many rubber balls.

Ganelon growled and swung balled fists, batting them aside in mid-leap. He soon discovered that their broad-shouldered little bodies were hard as wood, the outer layers of their epidermis so tough as to be almost petrified. It proved remarkably difficult to hurt the squalling little monsters, but he found their skulls could be cracked open if you pounded their heads against the stone slabs enough times. In quick succession he brained the first three or four who came within reach of his long arms.

They withdrew, squeaking and hissing ominously amongst themselves, eyeing him venomously. Ganelon rested, breathing easily, wishing he had not left the Silver Sword behind him in the Scarlet City. But there was no use in crying over lost weapons. The next time they rushed him he bent, pried a mighty slab out of the crumbling soil and hurled it at them, squashing three or four of them flat as stepped-on toads.

Glancing skywards, he wished the Bazonga bird would come.

They rushed him again, hissing like so many teakettles, jabbing at him with their stony spears. His criss-cross harness of black leather broke or deflected most of the spear-points, and the few scratches he did suffer hurt him scarcely at all. He grabbed up the first couple of wriggling little monster-men and tried to see how far he could throw them. Try as often as he could, the best he could do was about ten yards.

A change of tactics was needed here, obviously. If he simply stood here and let the little horrors come at him, they might wear him down before he had managed to extinguish all of them. Anti-life, of which the Death Dwarves were a prominent species, were of necessity remarkably difficult to kill, being not quite really alive in the first place.

He decided, after some thought, during which he managed to brain two more of the vile little creatures by hurling loose boulders at them, to make a sprint for the mountains. If he could get far enough above his pursuers, it should prove easy enough to drop big rocks on them, or perhaps trigger off an avalanche of respectable proportions.

With Ganelon, to think was to act. Whirling about, he sprang in the direction of the Vanishing Mountains, with as much speed as he could, considering the broken nature of the landscape. With a hissing cry, the green horde poured after him, waddling and hopping along at his heels.

It was no use; they could move faster than he over the broken slabs of tilted stone. In a few moments, a detachment of Dwarves had moved around in front of him, blocking him off.

He took his stand, and fought.

He was still doggedly knocking them about when they came upon him from behind, and beat him unconscious with stone clubs. Then, with many a spiteful kick in the ribs, the little green monsters trussed the unconscious Construct securely, and began dragging him off to their hidden lair. Within a few moments, save for the dead who lay scattered about, there was nothing on the plain of broken stones to show that a furious battle had been fought here—and had been lost.

# Book Two

~~~~~~~~~~~~~~~~~~~~~~~~~~~~~~~~~~~~

# *THE QUEEN OF RED MAGIC*

*The Scene:* The Country of the Death Dwarves; The Land of Red Magic; The Palace and City of Shai.

*New Characters:* The Enchantress Zelmarine; A Karjixian Tigerman; A Mentalist of Ning; Death Dwarves, Automatons, Courtiers, and Boys.

# 8.

# *SLAVES OF ZELMARINE*

If this was a prison cell, thought Ganelon Silvermane to himself, it was certainly the most comfortable one he had ever seen or heard of. Indeed, "comfortable" was hardly the *mot juste:* "luxurious" would be more like it.

The flooring consisted of scented fruitwoods, laid out in a complicated parquet, an arabesque of delicately-contrasting wood tones and grains. The windows, heavily barred though they were, were hung with sumptuous draperies. Thick carpets were soft underfoot, divans stood about piled with plump cushions, and small exquisite tabourets of carved Behemoth-tusk ivory (each table carved, of course, from a single tusk or portion of tusk) were scattered around the room. These bore a tempting variety of wines and liqueurs in cut-crystal decanters, platters of spiced meats, dainty pastries and fresh fruits. And the walls glowed with lambent tapestries of the sort for which the Spider Women of Yu are celebrated.

Galendil alone knows what the Death Dwarves would have done to him, had they been free to choose!* Just about the time he had come groggily back to consciousness, the little green men were turning their captive over to a squadron of Red Magic soldiers. They bore

---

* They would *not,* however, have eaten him: such forms of Anti-life commonly subsist on venom, acid, poison, excrement, ground glass, and less mentionable substances.

him on *Ornithohippus*-back due east a full day's ride, and into Shai, the capital of the Land of Red Magic.

It only confirmed what Silvermane had earlier heard from the vapor-veiled lips of the Illusionist, who considered the Red Enchantress a prime danger to the realms about. That is, she had recently brought under her will certain tribes of Dwarfland, which bordered upon her own dominions. He did not know whether the Enchantress had alerted the border tribes of Dwarfland to be on the look-out for a Construct of his description; or whether it was standard operating procedure for the little green horrors to seize upon all intruders across their borders and turn them over to the Red Magic legionnaires. Nor did it really matter.

His first experience of Zelmarine's country was not particularly interesting. The *Ornith* bore him along a winding, dusty road which meandered through rocky hills of crumbling shale, and across a plain of alkaline salt towards distant mountains. The *Ornith* itself he found more interesting than the dreary landscape through which it bore him.

*Ornithohippus* had only evolved into being about three-quarters of a million years before this time, and was thus a rank newcomer among the Gondwanish fauna. The bird horse strongly resembled an ostrich or emu, being devoid of wings, but it was a quadruped and somewhat bigger than the larger birds of our own day. The one the soldiers put him on was a handsome creature with snowy plumes and a long tapering crimson beak. It had a long graceful swan-neck, which it carried proudly arched, and from its pate a crest of nodding plumes streamed out behind it. Cantering on its four clawed feet, it moved with fluid grace and agility. *Orniths* were rarely used in Zermish, Ganelon's home-city, and he had never before been astride one of the lovely creatures.

The Red Magic legionnaires who conducted him to Shai were a surly, hard-faced lot, with copper-brown skins. They were clad in curious breastplates, gauntlets, helms, kilts and greaves made from stiff leather, lacquered a startling crimson. They rode heavily armed with sting-swords, dart-throwers, yarmaks, war hammers and pornoi, in whose use they seemed fully adept. Ganelon wisely decided resistance would be futile, if not fatal.

As they had approached Shai, the harsh landscape transformed itself into lush gardens. Doubtless, the Enchantress had employed her magic to clothe the terrain immediately adjacent to her capitol in verdure. They rode over arched bridges, across tinkling streams, through nodding groves of feather-trees. Marble statuary groups and ornamental gazebos lent a park-like flavor to the lovely landscape.

Shai itself turned out to be a miniature city of only a few thousand inhabitants. It was a splendid sight as they approached it, riding along a stone causeway across the limpid waters of an artificial lake: a graceful and artistic grouping of slender spires and minarets, placed in tasteful contrast to swelling onion-domes. The city was entirely built out of sparkling red glass* which flashed and glittered brilliantly in the dawn-light.

Entering the city by its sole gate, whose glassy barbican-towers were fantastically worked into flame-like points and flying buttresses, they traversed the miniature metropolis to the soaring cluster of pylons at its heart. This was, Ganelon assumed correctly, the Palace of the Queen of Red Magic. It consisted of nine spires of varying heights, interconnected by flying aerial bridges, with a spiral ramp enclosing the entire group.

The streets, squares and shops were virtually deserted, and the few persons they did pass on their way were a sullen-faced, dispirited lot with frightened faces and empty eyes, who shied away from the Red Magic legion. Most of the buildings they passed were soaring palaces and superb mansions whose fluted colonnades

---

* Stiffened, of course, to steely hardness by the use of Fire Magic, as had been used to toughen the precious metal of Ganelon's weapon, the Silver Sword. See the entry on "Magic" in the *Glossary of Unfamiliar Names and Terms* at the end of this book.

and impressive facades gleamed in the brilliance of dawn. The vistas of the city were breathtakingly lovely. But it seemed odd to the bronze giant that so many of the gorgeous glass palaces, although in perfect repair and kept immaculately cleaned and polished, seemed to be completely empty.

Shai was, he knew, a brand-new city which had arisen only in the past generation. The Queen of Red Magic herself was but newly come to Northern Yama-YamaLand, having arrived in these parts somewhat less than a century ago. Rumor had it that she was the last of a race of Red Amazons who had formerly inhabited the Cham Archipelago near Thoph in the remote, virtually unknown southwestern corner of the Supercontinent. Studying the Secret Sciences at the magician's college of Nembosch, she had discovered one of the nine-thousand ninety portals which gave entry into the Halfworld Labyrinth, a complex system of inter-dimensional conduits connecting several parts of this world with adjacent worlds and planes. This labyrinth, known to the scholars of legend as the "Cavern of a Thousand Perils," exited in the Mountains of the Death Dwarves. Emerging therefrom, Zelmarine had established her dominance over the eastern half of Dwarfland and announced her empire.

The Death Dwarves had, at first, fought furiously against her kingdom; conquered by her invincible scythe-armed Automatons, they withdrew into their mountains and eventually some of the border tribes fell under Zelmarine's dominance. She had employed the tireless vigor of her Automatons, together with the mineral strength and durance of the subservient Dwarves, to raise her capitol on the edges of the mountain country. She captured by magic whole village populations from the realms about to people her glass metropolis. This explained the cowed, subdued attitude of the few Shai citizens Ganelon had encountered on the way hither.

As for the Red Enchantress herself, he had not yet

enjoyed an audience with her, although he had glimpsed her once from a distance; the time she had paid a visit of state to the Hegemon of Zermish after Ganelon's victory in the Battle of Uth had brought to an end the invasion of the Indigons.* He was not exactly looking forward to the eventual interview with his captress, for from all descriptions she was a forceful, dynamic, voluptuous woman of imperious will and dominance—exactly the sort of person the simple, inexperienced young giant felt most uncomfortable with. But he had long known of her interest in him, although her reasons were still unknown to him. Indeed, shortly before he had left his home in Zermish to enter the service of the Illusionist of Nerelon, Zelmarine had attempted to purchase him from the Hegemon of his natal city. It was all rather ominous and uncomfortable.

But if this was the sort of captivity she inflicted upon her slaves, he thought to himself, it certainly wasn't hard to endure! He hadn't eaten such sumptuous meals since leaving the enchanted palace of Nerelon, and his surroundings were of a degree of luxury he had never before enjoyed. He ate heartily, drank deeply, and slept magnificently in an emperor-sized bed piled high with silken pillows, under a gold-lamé canopy.

During the day, however, there was nothing much to do. The door to his prison suite was a gigantic slab of sculptured wood whose exquisite carving and detailwork did not conceal the fact that it was tougher than iron and weighed a ton or two. And, each time his meals were served to him and he managed to catch a glimpse of the corridor beyond, he could see that the only entrance to his apartment was heavily guarded by twenty motionless but sentient metal Automatons.

Some of the hollow metal men had arms which terminated in scythes or hooks, others in sledges, powerdrills and swordblades. From his former experiences

---

* For a narrative of these events, see Chapters 6 to 8 of the First Book of the Epic, entitled *The Warrior of World's End*, DAW Books, 1974.

back at Nerelon, where the Illusionist had maintained
a few Automatons of his own for heavy work around
the palace, he knew the enchanted creatures were virtually indestructible. He had little or no chance of
fighting his way through such a heavy number, despite
his own very-much-more-than-human strength and
vigor.

Well, he decided philosophically, if one has to be enslaved by Zelmarine the Enchantress, at least durance
vile under conditions of such lavishness and comfort
can be suffered pleasantly.

# 9.

# THE FEAST OF
# THE FALLING MOON

On the second evening of Ganelon's captivity in Shai, he met his captress at last.

The occasion was an annual feast which, in certain heathen and outlandish regions of Gondwane, such as that from which the Red Queen came, shamans and warlocks make sacrifice in order to propitiate the Moon. It should perhaps be explained that, in this distant Eon of the future, the gravitational action and tidal forces have slowed the Moon in her ancient orbit to a point where she had drawn perilously near to the surface of Old Earth—very much nearer than she has come in our own age. Some fear, indeed, that she will ere long reach Roche's Limit and be torn apart in the grip of these forces, burying Gondwane beneath millions of tons of meteoric debris; others, perhaps less scientifically knowledgeable, assume the Moon will fall to Earth, destroying the entire planet in the collision. No one knows for sure when the calamity will befall (if I may be permitted the indulgence of an inadvertent pun), or into which category the nature of the cataclysm will go, but if you could see how threateningly huge and ominously zigzagged with cracks the face of the enormous satellite looked from the Gondwanian surface, you would certainly understand how imminent seemed the peril. Few believed such sacrificial feasts could avert the cosmic catastrophe, but a bit of propitiation never hurts.

Hook-handed Automatons clanked stiffly into Ganelon's suite, depositing festive robes of gold and scarlet cloth, and stood motionless but wary while the giant unwillingly donned the raiment. They then escorted him from the room and, by a succession of spiral stairways, into a magnificent hall where the Red Queen sat enthroned on a chair of sparkling crystal, high above her courtiers.

The room itself was cruciform in shape, and nine storys deep. A forest of glass pillars of mammoth girth supported the roof which was transparent, permitting the silver glory of the lunar radiance—transmuted to a flood of crimson light by passage through the tinted glass—to fall in splendor upon the festive assembly. At the point where the two arms of the cross joined, was a central rotunda, in the very center of which the throne of the Red Queen sat atop a many-stepped dais like a miniature pyramid.

Red Magic legionnaires led him through the assembled feasters to the bottom-most step of this dais, and for the first time Ganelon Silvermane and the Enchantress of Shai met face to face. For a long moment, neither moved or spoke, both stared thoughtfully at each other, like swordsmen measuring an opponent's skill before engaging their blades.

The Red Queen was a magnificent woman, nearly naked, her splendid body adorned with flashing gems and plaques of precious metals, a plumed tiara glittering upon her brow. At the height of a good seven feet, she stood very nearly as tall as Ganelon himself. She was built to scale, with powerful though feminine arms, bare shoulders and long, sleek, well-muscled but shapely legs.

The most remarkable thing about her was, of course, her famous coloration, from whence she derived her sobriquet. That is to say, the Red Enchantress was really *red*. Her entire body was colored a brilliant, not unattractive shade of crimson; her long waving tresses and arched, sardonic brows were also crimson, but of a shade slightly darker than the rest of her. Her eyes were of a red so dark as to be almost, but not quite, black. Her lips and the protuberant nipples of her superb breasts were of a darker red, almost plum-purple. When she smiled, Ganelon discovered that even her teeth were red, as were the whites of her eyes.

She was superb! Queenly, imperious, she towered head and shoulders above most of the men at her court, with a magnificent bosom, bare beneath glittering ropes of diamonds, a narrow waist and full, swelling hips and thighs. Tiny jewelled slippers clung to her feet and an immense cut diamond the size of a walnut flashed in her navel. When she spoke, as she did now, her voice was a low, liquid murmur, purring and seductive, but with a man's deep-chested timbre in it, and the steely ring of command, too.

It was the sort of voice that was accustomed to being obeyed.

With a dramatic gesture, she rose suddenly to her feet, towering above them all. The mumble of low-voiced conversation in the hall ceased instantly and silence stretched taut.

Then she came swaying down the tier of steps to his level, extending one hand whose crimson fingers dazzled with diamonds.

"Ganelon Silvermane! Be you welcome to the court of Shai. Consider yourself, not my prisoner, but—my guest!"

The Illusionist of Nerelon would have been flabbergasted at what Ganelon did next. For, summoning from within himself a courtliness none could have guessed him to possess, the young giant bowed and, taking her long fingers in his own, brushed the backs of her fingers with his lips. She smiled a delighted, warm smile, her full, lush lips curving.

"Seat yourself here," she said, gesturing to a cushion upon the lower steps, "in the place that is reserved for heroes. And join our lunar festival, with honor and welcome!"

Ganelon nodded, sat tailor-fashion on the silken pillow and let himself be served by one of the Automatons who stalked on clanking feet among the courtiers,

refilling a goblet here and presenting platters of food
there.

Deliberately turning his attention from the Enchantress, he feigned interest in the other guests, who
were seated on cushions in rows before long, low tabourets of dark wood. They were certainly a motley crew,
thought he: among them he spied a Voormish clans-
man in his long burnoose, one or two of the Tigermen
of Karjixia, a rather glum and lumpish-looking creature that seemed to be one of the Halfmen of Thaad,
and a Horxite ecclesiastic or two in black robes and
gilt-paper headdress. There were also Quentishmen
and Ixlanders, a few visiting dignitaries from Oryx,
Pergamoy and Sabdon in the Hegemony (or so their
tartan sashes suggested), and a horde chieftain from
the Dominions of Akoob Khan in the far east, to say
nothing of a painted savage in feather-robes who could
only have come from the Kakkawakka Islands. Beyond these, a lone, now-homeless Airmaster in glittering blue tights with winged crystal helm, and a couple
of woeful-looking, long-nosed and stilt-legged Quaylies,
the remainder of the Queen's guests and courtiers origi-
nated in lands whereof he knew nothing.

For the most part, this variegated company ate,
drank, dozed, chatted or caroused, ogled the dancing
girls and flirted. They paid Ganelon very little attention beyond an occasional oblique and cunning glance
of surreptitious appraisal. Few, if any, seemed to know
who or what he was; it was probably taken for granted
that he was a newcomer to the ranks of royal favorites.

The Horxite priest sat stiffly and did not deign to
look in his direction, and the two Tigermen, a scruffy
duo with the look of outlawry about them, ignored
everyone else and devoted themselves to the meat-
platters on the tabouret before them. Seated quite far
from all the others sat a Death Dwarf, considerably
larger, burlier and more intelligent-looking than the
ones which had attacked Silvermane on the slopes of
the Vanishing Mountains. This creature was clad in
linked plates of shining steel and wore a coronet of iron

spikes upon his wart-studded bald brows. Ganelon learned later that he was Drng, chieftain of the tribes subservient to Zelmarine. Ganelon looked at the platter of broken glass and the thick ceramic goblet of bubbling acid from which the little horror imbibed gluttonously, and shuddered: no wonder he was not seated with the other guests!

The feast had obviously been in progress ever since Moonrise, the sacrifice was long since over and two ritually-slain Androsphinxes were impaled on the Moon Altar. Ganelon glanced, then looked away in distaste; he might be only a simple, untutored oaf from the back-alleys of Zermish, but he did not believe that the ceremonial execution of fabulous monsters could avert the doom of the Falling Moon. And, in his opinion, anyone who did was lacking somewhat in intelligence.

He was not particularly hungry, only picked at his food, and drank lightly from the sparkling beverages set before him. There was no point in trying to examine his nutriment for the presence of narcotics; since he was completely in the power of Queen Zelmarine, she could drug him in any number of ways, at any time she wished to. With an elaborate pretence of indifference, he merely toyed with his food.

Dancing-girls, their stark nudity veiled only in that their sinuous bodies had been rubbed with adhesive, then sprinkled with dust-of-gold, undulated in the aisles between the rows of feasters. The thud and whiffle of small drums, the tootle and whine of pipes, came from musicians seated in the shadow of the nearer pillars.

Only one individual was seated on the steps of the dais in greater proximity to Zelmarine than himself. This was a lean, sour-faced personage in tight, narrow robes of eye-blinding indigo, with a silver hat and jangling bracelets which adorned his long bony wrists. His skin was sallow and umber, his large eyes black, fiery and magnetic. He seemed to be staring at Ganelon with an intensity that was almost rude, so Silvermane returned it, stare for stare.

Zelmarine, who had been covertly studying Silvermane's every expression and movement from behind her thick lashes, noticed this and spoke in her clear, low voice that had almost a growl in it.

"Permit me to make you known, Ganelon Silvermane, to my aide and confidant, Varesco, one of the Mentalists of Ning. He provides me with invaluable assistance in my researches on the human brain, a subject in which the Ningevite savants have attained to a mastery far surpassing my own."

Ganelon nodded briefly at the blue-robed Mind Worshipper, who returned it with a curt nod of equal brevity, and thereafter devoted his full attentions to his wine-cup.

At the conclusion of the feast, Zelmarine descended to where Ganelon had politely come to his feet, and gave him another of those lush, delighted smiles.

"I trust my servitors are doing all that is within their power to make your stay in our court comfortable," she said demurely. He bowed, and said quietly that the enforced inactivity wearied him, since he was used to violent exercise.

"If I might be permitted to work-out with your guardsmen, I would be grateful," he said somberly.

"Certainly!" She turned to a burly-shouldered, deep-chested officer, his red-lacquered leather armor crested and gilt with decorations of rank, who had been seated at the nearest tabouret. He had gotten to his feet, as had all the throng, when she herself had risen from her crystal throne. "Colonel Turmus, will you see to it that our honored guest is given the freedom of the exercise-yard? Under proper escort, of course!"

"It shall be done, my lady," the officer said, saluting by touching his left shoulder with the palm of his right hand.

"Farewell, then, for the moment," the Red Queen said to Silvermane. He bowed again and thanked her,

whereupon she smiled and sauntered off, hips swaying languidly as she strolled down the aisle between
the tables, to vanish from the hall behind the thick
velvet draperies which masked a doorway between two
pillars.

The throng stood in utter silence while she moved
gracefully from the room.

Ganelon was a little surprised to notice that, while
from the front she had worn at least a modicum of
jewelry, from the back she looked completely naked
from the nape of her neck to the heels of her gem-
twinkling slippers.

The bronze giant, slightly disconcerted, turned his
eyes away from the plump rondure of her perfectly-
proportioned buttocks. In so doing, he chanced to look
in the direction of the lean Ningevite Mentalist.

Varesco was staring after the Enchantress with avid
hunger in his burning eyes. Oblivious to all else but the
languid swaying of her nude back and bottom, her long,
lithe legs, he watched with fascination glittering in his
black, hot eyes. He wet his thin lips a little with a
pointed tongue as she strolled out of sight.

Ganelon frowned heavily. The tensions and under-
currents at this weird court were beyond his limited
sophistication. How he wished the old Illusionist could
be here to advise him on his words and actions!

# 10.
# *GRRFF THE XOMBOLIAN*

Bright and early the next morning Ganelon rose from his sumptuous bed, breakfasted lightly, and under a heavy guard of clanking Automatons, went forth into the exercise-yard of the Red Legion to work out with the local weaponry. For the occasion he had put aside the silken gowns of the wardrobe which Zelmarine had furnished, in favor of his plain, worn war-harness of black leathern straps and the swash-topped boots.

The Red Legion was quartered in long rows of bar-racks behind the Palace of Red Magic, screened from view by tall, flowering tamerinkus trees. The exercise-yard itself was spacious in the extreme, almost the size of a gladiatorial arena, with stadium seats in a half-circle around it. There was a variety of gear wherewith the warriors of the Legion practiced daily, in prepara-tion for war, invasion, riot or insurrection.

The officer who had been in the forefront of the feast was there to observe the foreign giant as he worked out. This Colonel—"Turmus," the Red Queen had called him—was stout and aging, with grizzled, close-cropped hair and a ruddy face; his eyes were cold, ice-gray, unfriendly. He nodded imperceptibly in reply to Ganelon's greeting, wordlessly indicating racks of weaponry and instruments wherewith the visitor pre-sumably might make free—under constant supervision, of course.

Ganelon looked the racks over approvingly. There

were swords of every size and description; spears, javelins, pikes, billhooks, hammers and axes, yarmaks and bows, volusks, discus-dags, war-boomerangs, and other examples of weaponry familiar to him from his service in the militia of Zermish. There were also several kinds of war-instruments unfamiliar to him; he selected one of these, a throwing-trident with hollow glass prongs, and hefted its weight curiously, wondering just how it was used.

"Ho, there, friend! You seem unaccustomed to the mer-spike; if so, let Grrff caution you to avoid fracturing the tips of the triple point," said a husky, rough-edged voice from behind him. He turned to see a powerful Karjixian Tigerman stripped to his barred, tawny fur, clad only in black-leather groincup and high-strapped sandals.

"Thanks for the advice," said Ganelon. "As a matter of fact, I've never seen one of these before: how are they used?"

The Tigerman took it in his paw and upended it. "The Merfolk of the Second Inland Sea use these when hunting sea snakes," he growled. "The prongs alone are frangible, containing nerve poison; the sea people hurl these like spears at the aquatic reptiles; they break on their scaly backs, injecting venom which causes paralysis. Galendil only knows why the Red Bitch has her soldiers train in their use, unless mayhap she plans to add the Inland Sea to her cursed empire, with all the rest!"

Ganelon pricked up his ears at the expletive. They were some yards away from where Colonel Turmus stood watching with cold, sullen eyes, and the Karjixian had spoken in gruff, low tones which had probably not been overheard.

"I gather you are no friend to Zelmarine?" he inquired quietly. "But weren't you at the moon-festival last night?"

The Tigerman gave a snarling laugh, and spit into the sawdust, wrinkling up his whiskery snout. "Not Grrff, big man! He shares a cell in the prison wing of the Palace, albeit one slightly less snug and comfy than yours, if rumor is truth for once. If fellow-country-men o' Grrff's were at the feast, the curs were rene-gades. Outcasts or renegades!"

Ganelon digested this news with considerable inter-est. It is always to the future benefit of a prisoner to make genial contact with his fellow-captives, it occurred to him. He introduced himself; the Tigerman blinked with surprise.

"The warrior who rallied the troops at Uth and broke the Indigons last year?" he asked. His yellow cat-eyes glowed with pleasure and his furry ears twitched "Well-met, then, big man! I am by name Grrff, a war-chief of the Farrowl clan of Xombol. Grrff led a party up against the blue vermin when they came swarming down out of the north, shortly ere they turned east at the Crystal Mountains to stampede against your town of Zermish. They were mighty fighters, and tough to kill; my hand, warrior!"

Ganelon took the furry paw and squeezed it in friendly fashion. He measured the Tigerman with curi-ous eyes, and liked what he saw. The Xombolian only came to his shoulder, of course, but his mighty torso rippled with bulging thews beneath the short nap of his orange fur, which was striped with black and ivory. He had met Tigermen before, and he generally liked them. He said as much.

"I was in Xombol not long ago, with friends," he added.

"Oh, aye? How are things there? Poor Grrff's been caged up here since the damnable Indigons crushed his warmen and left him cut off from any chances of homeward retreat. There was nowhere else to go but east, damn the filthy luck, and of course poor Grrff ran into an ambush in Dwarfland and the little mon-sters sold him into bondage here. What the Red Bitch wants with him is simple treason—knowledge of the guard-posts and troop-disposal about my King's capitol; and as Grrff will not speak, she pens him here in du-rance, hoping to break his spirit!"

"King Vrowl? My master is a good friend of his, and we were guests in Xombol palace on the visit I told you of," said Ganelon. They exchanged a few more words, but then Colonel Turmus, who had been distracted by a messenger, noticed the two captives conversing in low tones. He sent a pair of Automatons clanking over to separate them.

Till noon, Ganelon and Grrff the Tigerman exercised in the sun, using weapon after weapon against straw dummies as hacking-posts, but too widely apart for further words. When they left the field, however, they waved a friendly goodbye to each other, and exchanged conspiratorial grins and winks.

In the very stronghold of his enemies, Ganelon Silvermane had found a friend.

Somehow, the future looked a little brighter for that.

Every morning thereafter, Silvermane looked forward to his hours in the exercise-yard. Not only did he enjoy the opportunity to stretch and toughen his muscles, and to increase and develop his skills with the weapons of war, but he anticipated the furtive pleasures of conversation with the Tigerman. Indeed, he and his new-found friend managed to talk a bit, for Turmus was very often absent on his Queen's business, and the Automatons stationed about the field to guard against his escape were too stupid or too uncaring to keep them apart.

It was from Grrff that he learned something about the ambitions of the Red Enchantress. "She's a cunning, unscrupulous, intelligent, ruthless female," growled the Tigerman. "She has notions to incorporate the Realm of the Nine Hegemons and the Voormish tribesmen, together with Dwarfland and such city-states about as Oym, Chx, and Abbergathy—to say nothing of Quay, Ixland, the country of the Holy Horxites and Grrff's own beloved homeland of Karjixia, into one gigantic Empire. With her Redness, of course, as the Empress. She already has gotten a hold on some of the Dwarves, and she has managed to intimidate the Hegemons of

Pergamoy, Sabdon and your own town of Zermish;
Jargo's next on the agenda, I fancy."

"But how does she plan to manage it? She doesn't
have much of an army."

Grrff shrugged, his nape-fur ruffling at the thought.
"Don't put down the Red Legion till you've seen them
fight, big man! Anyway, she's got some of the Dwarf-
tribes under her thumb, and you know what ferocious
fighters those green devils can be. Then she's got her
scythe-armed Automatons, of course. There must be a
thousand of them by now, maybe twice that number.
And more a-building every day, in the underground
factories. Oh, you didn't know about the factories?
Well, Shai is a pretty place, if you like glass—and if
you care for red; I'm sick to death of the color myself,
after all these months—but didn't you notice how many
of the pretty buildings are mere facades, with nobody
living inside them? What's on the surface is to fool
visiting ambassadors and Outlander spies. Underground, it's all grimy manufactories, busily turning
out the tools of war, and hordes of those metal men
that can't be killed. Thirty a day come rolling off the
assembly lines, Grrff hears; but that may be only prison
scuttlebutt . . ."

Ganelon rubbed his jaw reflectively.

"My master, the magician of Nerelon, knows a lot
about her and considers her a powerful threat to Northern YamaYamaLand. I wonder if he knows about the
underground war works."

"Nerelon, eh? Grrff's heard of him—a great friend of
King Vrowl and an ally of his royal father, if we're
talking about the same Illusionist. Skinny little geezer,
keeps himself covered and gloved, and wears perfumed
smoke to hide his face? The same one, then. He was
also a good friend to my ancestors, in the previous
two or three reigns."

"Really? Goodness, I didn't know he was as old as
all that; but you can never tell with magicians, can
you?"

The Tigerman grinned, revealing strong white fangs

set in bright pink gums. "You can't, and that's a fact. Grrff can recall one time he had a run-in with a troublesome wizard, up Thazarian mountain country. Fellow just came down one day, riding on a Phlygûl. Planned to build his tower and lord it over some of the Karjixian villages down that way. The King dispatched poor Grrff on a punitive expedition, at the head of a thousand warriors, to pound some sense into his skull. Turned out to be a nice old fellow, after all, and willing to listen to reason . . . a thousand war-axes speak mighty eloquent, I guess . . . The whole trouble was, the wizard was so old he remembered Karjixia before we Tiger-folk evolved and got ourselves civilized. He thought the whole country was still just wild jungleland, with nobody to own it! Fellow must have been all of fifty thousand years old! Name of Clesper Volphotex, as I recall. Nice-enough old human, once you talked some sense into him . . ."

Ganelon nodded absently, not really listening. His brow was furrowed with puzzlement.

"I wonder what she wants with me?" he mused. "Master was never sure about that. I don't know anything about the defences of the Hegemonic cities; no war-chief, I was only a militiaman. Why do you suppose she has me locked up in such a luxurious cell, inviting me to feasts and all?"

"Grrff doesn't know, big man," growled the Tigerman. Then, ominously, he added: "But he's a hunch you're going to find out before the world's much older . . ."

# 11.
# *THE SUPERWOMAN SPEAKS*

That very night, as it turned out, Ganelon got an inkling of what the Red Queen wanted of him.

He was invited to partake of a private supper in the seclusion of the Queen's own suite. The apartments of Zelmarine were situated high in the tallest of the elfin spires of ruby glass, to which he was escorted by more of the omnipresent metal men who went clinking and clanking along, looking for all the world like suits of old-fashioned armor with nobody inside them.

The dining-chamber was open to the star-lit night, crystal panes folded back to let the evening breezes float in, rustling the gorgeous draperies and sending the flames a-flickering on tall red tapers. Below, a glittering vista of Shai by starlight spread out like a jewelled carpet, with the grim, ragged masses of the Mountains of the Death Dwarves beyond, blocking off the world to the north.

The Enchantress wore a thin gown, a mere tissue of ebony silk, on this occasion, and her glistening tresses were caught up in a loose net of jacinths. Curled in a nest of cushions, she lazily waved him to a seat beside her. Across from the low crystal table, the Mentalist of Ning sat, sour-eyed and glowering. A casual light repast of sparkling, effervescent wine in fluted goblets, plates of crisp Garongaland salad bedabbled with creamy swickleberry dressing, tidbits of broiled cave-fish swimming in pepper-sauce, lay spread out on the table. Ganelon was invited to help himself.

The conversation was casual, wandering from topic to topic without ever quite coming to rest. The Enchantress found several excuses to touch Ganelon's arm or wrist lightly, and her warm thigh brushed his under the table whenever she reached for a delicacy.

He sat there, stolidly ignoring the deep cut of her gown and seemingly oblivious to the warm, musky perfume that rose from the cleavage of her full breasts. She spoke in her deep, husky voice, and it sent shivers up his spine. The witchery of starlight glimmered on her thick, dark hair, and a warm glow shone in her large, lovely, slightly tilted eyes. Every word chimed with faintly seductive music; every touch was a caress.

Blue-robed Varesco sat hunched across the table, chewing on his thin lip and hating him. Ganelon pretended not to notice the open invitation in Zelmarine's every word and glance, or the overpowering allure of her presence.

Or was it affectation? Perhaps he was truly oblivious to the pull of this woman, this superwoman, this sorceress who was half a witch and half a goddess. Often, back in Zermish, his mother had speculated over his lack of interest in the nubile street-girls of the neighborhood, who had clustered about him like cats drawn to tempting bait during the years of adolescence. His master had once discussed the problem with Phlesco, Ganelon's adoptive father, cautioning him not to expect the usual wedding and fatherhood. Ganelon was a Construct, not a True Human. The Time Gods had designed him for some unknown purpose of their own, breeding him in their tissue vats; and perhaps the design had not included the normal masculine glands, emotions, instincts. It was too soon to tell; "born" fully-grown from the Ardelix Vault, Ganelon was about twelve years old, as far as the drives of manhood were concerned.

The Enchantress purred silkenly, her emotions rising at the nearness of the bronze giant. She panted, her superb bosom rising and falling, her blood afire. All of her magnificent womanliness she poured into every sidelong glance of her glorious eyes, into every pout or smile of her lush mouth. The magic of her fleshly loveliness had captured hundreds of men before, many of them only partially human: surely, this oafish bumpkin of a Zermishman was not proof against her charms, where princes, heroes and Mysteriarchs had succumbed!

The wine she urged on him contained a secret aphrodisiac; the musky perfume she wore was a heady intoxicant blended by an alchemist in her service; the dishes from which he ate were mixed with subtle narcotics designed to arouse the desires of the male.

Through it all, Ganelon sat like a statue of cold, adamantine bronze, noticing nothing, feeling nothing. When Varesco rose at her signal to make his reluctant departure, she flashed him a fiery glance; she knew the gaunt, lust-maddened Mentalist was enslaved by her: why, then, was Ganelon invulnerable to her lure?

As they sat alone together, she began to speak. Her deep, husky voice began to spin a web of enchantment about him. She spoke of the many lands of Northern Yama YamaLand, of how they were divided by old traditions, ancient enmities, and long centuries of independence; she told him how they wasted their strength in futile strife, one state against the other, and of how mighty would be their destiny were they to combine in one gigantic alliance. One empire, built of many kingdoms (she purred huskily in his ear) could in time enlist all of the scattered shreds and scraps of dwindling True Humanity under one imperial banner, to master the destiny of Gondwane itself. Should not the Last Age be one of ultimate and immortal glory for humanity? Should not the terminal remnants of mankind stand together in one last, titanic empire, to startle and amaze the world in the Twilight of Time?

Snuggling closer to him on the silken divan, she argued that it would take a superhuman combination of will, intellect and daring to create such a magnificent achievement. Such a being as, she averred, for instance—herself. Although not a True Human, she nurtured vast, illimitable respect and admiration for the deeds of earlier times and former civilizations; unlike so many Quasi-humans, she was a devout Humanophile, and yearned to guide the Last Men in one final, glorious enterprise which could fittingly stand as the ultimate culmination of human history . . .

But, although her powers were great, her ambition and sense of dedication splendid, she was, alas, only mortal. Such empires, constructed by a single genius, tend to swiftly erode upon their leader's demise, crumbling from internal strains and stresses. The only way such an empire could be built to last for ages, perhaps even unto the end of the world, was through the establishment of a dynasty. Zelmarine must, therefore, seek out a male whose strength, greatness and courage were as superhuman as her own. Casting him many a meaningful sidewise glance, she bemoaned the lack of supermen in this decadent age. Should such a supermortal appear, she vowed, her lush bosom rising and falling with the tumult of her emotions, he could take her by storm: she would yield everything to his ardent assault. And that included her superb body and her unrivalled capacities for carnal pleasure . . .

Ganelon nodded noncommittally and asked if he could pour her more wine. He sipped the drink moodily, as if unaware that the wine was heavily laced with a potent aphrodisiac. She eyed him furiously, chewing on her lower lip. He seemed as unaware that her heaving breasts were only inches from his hand, her panting lips only a reach away, as if they were separated by continents, conversing by televisor.

The intimate supper came to its inconclusive end. Automatons escorted Silvermane back to his sumptuous cell. Varesco reentered the suite at her summons, gloating with his hot eyes, a smirk faintly visible on his thin, starved mouth. She released a tempest of tears, striding up and down the room smashing furniture with blows of her powerful fists, shattering vases in her fury.

Barely able to conceal his delight at the indifference which his rival displayed towards the alluring charms of the Enchantress, Varesco strove to discredit him yet further in the eyes of the humiliated Queen of Red Magic.

"Perhaps the fleshly lusts of the champion lie in . . . ah . . . more epicene directions?" he purred. She bathed him in a furious glare; then her glorious eyes were veiled in silken lashes as she pondered the possibility. Although remote, it was of course conceivable. It would at least relieve her humiliation, were it to be demonstrated that Ganelon Silvermane scorned not her, but her entire gender, favoring more effete partners.

"Test his vulnerabilities therein," she commanded brusquely, before sweeping from the room. Varesco bowed and smiled covertly as she receded from him. Thereafter, the servitors who brought Ganelon's meals were slender youths with fawn-like eyes, full-lipped pouting mouths, sleek thighs and tender buttocks. Although they presented themselves before him in every variety of dress from feminine garments, lace lingerie, leather suits to even weirder forms of apparel—as well as complete nudity—the Construct paid them little attention. He never so much as ventured a caress, although the parade of beautiful boys made it obvious that they were amenable to his pleasures, and were at his disposal, whatever form it might take. In desperation, Zelmarine exposed Silvermane to old men and women, animals, prepubescent children of all four sexes, and every conceivable kind of Subhuman, Quasi-human, and Non-human, including, of course, the Pseudo-women of Chuu. Although actually a form of vegetable life, these Pseudo-women were complete duplicates of human females in all capacities save that of reproduction*; they had been bred to incredible seduc-

---

* They reproduced their kind through bud or graft instead of birth. It will be recalled that Ganelon's own foster-mother, Iminix, was of their kind.

tive beauty through ages of scientific horticulture. To one and all, Silvermane remained aloof and unresponsive.

The private dinner proved to be but the first of many such, during which the Enchantress presented herself before Silvermane in a bewildering variety of raiment, each gown more ravishingly beautiful and more revealing than the one before. The beverages served to the Construct contained half the narcotics and aphrodisiacs in the pharmacopoeia. The final supper of the sequence saw Zelmarine clothed in naught but a dusting of powdered emeralds, and the wine heady with sufficient aphrodisiacs to madden with lust the denizens of an entire monastery.

Ganelon remained celibate and disinterested to the end. But Zelmarine had not yet given up and felt confident she could wear him down with time.

# 12.

# *ISTROBIAN'S FLYING KAYAK*

While the Red Queen strives to seduce Ganelon Silvermane with her wiles and blandishments, let us return to Chx and learn how the Illusionist, Xarda, and Prince Erigon have fared in the meanwhile.

Finding the Bazonga bird gone, as they did during their quick visit to the Hospice of the Eleven Cardinal Virtues, after making their midnight escape from the Administratium, put a severe crimp in their plans. It makes it more difficult, escaping on foot than by air. For one thing, you can put many leagues between you and your eventual pursuers when you fly. Afoot, however, is quite another matter.

"Surely, magister, the Chxians will not awaken from their nocturnal fit of criminality to discover our escape before dawn," argued the Sirix of Jemmerdy. "By then, in sooth, we shall be far away from Chx."

"Yes; but not as far as I could wish," grumbled the old magician testily. "Whatever could have possessed that pesky Bird to break her tether and fly off on her own? It just isn't like her to be so thoughtless and uncaring . . ."

The Prince of Valardus had been staring uncomprehendingly from one to the other as they talked. He did not, of course, understand to whom they were referring, since Ganelon Silvermane was the only missing member of their company, insofar as he knew.

He cleared his throat tentatively.

"Ahem! Is it, ah, a mode of transport you discuss?"

he inquired. Nodding brusquely, the Illusionist curtly described the brazen animated vehicle which had been both their steed and their companion on previous adventures. The puzzlement cleared from the Prince's handsome features.

"Ah!" he exclaimed. "An aerial device, then. In that case, pray permit me to offer you the services of my aerial kayak."

"An aerial kayak?" asked the Illusionist, surprised. "How fortunate! But how do you come to be in possession of the craft, which is, unless I am mistaken, an invention of Istrobian, the celebrated sorcerer of an earlier epoch?"

"It is indeed Istrobian's flying kayak to which I refer," said Erigon smilingly. "My late mother was a distant descendent of his, and it has long been in the possession of her family, passing thus by simple inheritance to me. As the celestial vessel travels more swiftly than could any mode of land transport, whether on *ornith* or *nguamodon,* I selected the vessel from the treasure-vault of Valardus-palace, employing it to travel swiftly and in comparative comfort to the nearby realms."

"But where is the miraculous vehicle now? Surely, the Ethical Triumvirs have purloined it—" began Xarda, but the young Prince cut off her flow of words with a lifted palm.

"It is here, in the very Hospice in whose courtyard we now stand," he smiled. "I parked it in the stables, securely tethered against any possibility of theft by use of a sentient rope. Having paid the Inn-keeper a cube of virgin copper for rental of the stable stall, and since, during the daylight hours, the Chxians are scrupulously honest, it is no doubt still tethered within."

"But *at night*—" began Xarda.

"At night, m'lady, the criminal Chxians have more notable malefactions to commit than theft of a stabled steed! Come, let us investigate."

He led them to the long row of stables. Within lay damp coolness, the odors of mouldy straw, the not-

unpleasant muskiness of *ornith* turds and *nguamodon*
droppings—and the kayak!

It was a four-seater, built like a long, slim canoe,
with a blade-thin point at either terminus. The seats
were all in a row down the mid-section of the craft, one
after the other like peas in a pod; and, kayak-like, the
bright blue fabric which was stretched tightly over the
light frame of the craft could be laced snugly about the
waist of the passengers. About thirty feet from stem to
stern, the craft hovered four or five feet above the
straw-strewn packed earth which floored the stable. It
was held tightly by a glassy, odd-looking rope which resembled a fat, lucent worm.

"What holds it up?" asked the Illusionist, entranced
with delight. "Our own Bazonga is impregnated with
*yxium* crystals, which resist gravity—"

"Nothing so complicated," said Erigon, shaking his
head. " 'Tis said that the sorcerer Istrobian wrought
the framework of the craft from the metal found in a
fallen star, but the savants of Valardus pooh-pooh this
as mere mythography, arguing that the thing which fell
was a fragment of the Moon itself—"

"A meteorite?"  ·

"If you wish to call it that," said the Prince in his
friendly, unargumentative manner. "At any rate, the
metal yearns for its lunar home—"

"Ah, of course!" said the Illusionist with satisfaction. "A well-known property of *dianium*\*—but pray
continue your intriguing discourse, Prince."

"Thank you. As I was saying, the metal yearns for
its lunar home, and seeks ever to return thence
. . . the gravity of Old Earth, however, proves
stronger than the pull of homesickness. It renders it
somewhat more than weightless. The metal of the ribs
is ferrous, hence magnetic, and the kayak is believed
to ride the magnetic lines of force about our planet."

---

\* Again I must refer the interested reader to the Glossary at the
end of the book. I simply cannot impede the headlong pace of my
narrative with lengthy explanations of each unfamiliar term.

"Subtle and ingenious," marvelled the old magician. "That Istrobian was a wonder-worker, in sooth! 'Tis far simpler than our beloved Bird . . ."

"But why the blue fabric?" asked Xarda.

"Oiled and enamelled, it keeps off the rain and the night-damps," explained Prince Erigon, "which would cause the moon-metal to rust, in time consuming the vessel utterly. Let me untie the craft and we can be off before any roving band of crazed and criminal Chxians chances upon us."

Murmurring low cooing sounds like a half-strangled dove, he approached the thick glassy rope which bound the floating kayak to the beams which upheld the stable roof. One end of the sentient rope lifted warningly at his approach, swaying from side to side like a cobra. But the tether seemed to recognize its master's tone, or perhaps his touch, and soon relaxed as he stroked and patted it. At his signal they clambered with some difficulty into the bucket-like seats, the kayak straining skyward all the while. Erigon himself was the last to spring lightly aboard the craft, bearing with him the coil of sentient rope which had wound itself about his upper chest and shoulders like a friendly tame boa constrictor.

Foot-pedals controlled the aerial craft. Manipulating them, Erigon eased the floating craft out into the courtyard under the blazing stars. They were unobserved. From the street beyond came happy cries, drunken singing and the jingle of shattering glass. The Chxians were busily in pursuit of their nocturnal pleasures.

Instructing them in the mode by which the kayak fabric could be drawn snugly about their waists and secured, the Prince sent the kayak arrowing skywards. Rooftops swung below the kayak's keel; towers and spires of scarlet stone whizzed by; soon the mad city of Chx fell behind, swallowed in night's gloom, save for the ruddy glow of several burning buildings.

"Whither now, magister?" asked Erigon, cupping his hands around his mouth and shouting the question.

The Illusionist shouted back that he had no idea where Ganelon might have gone, once he had managed to escape from the Administratium.

"What about your Third Eye, prithee?" sang the clear soprano of the girl knight above the wind, which snatched her words away. The Illusionist peered about, then shrugged.

"From this height I should be able to detect his Auric pattern, were he anywhere in this city. Evidently, he is not."

"I can't understand why the big lug would just go off and leave us in jail," sang Xarda with some asperity. "He may be stupid, but he was always loyal!"

"Perhaps he had no voice in the matter," replied the Illusionist, whose agile wits had perceived something like the truth in the fact that the Bazonga and Silvermane were both inexplicably absent. He knew the ungainly and absurdly motherly Bird was devoted to the simple youth.

"Well, where would he have most likely gone, had he been able to choose?" asked Prince Erigon. Xarda shrugged angrily: "Over the border, I guess, towards Jemmerdy. That was where we were all heading."

"Yes, but does Ganelon know in which direction Jemmerdy lies?" inquired the Illusionist. "The dear boy is not the brightest creature that ever trod Old Earth, you know!"

"Well, please, someone make up their mind. Tell me in which direction to fly," begged the Prince of Valardus.

"Oh, very well! Just fly in an ever-widening circle, with Chx in the middle, until I am able to spy Ganelon's aura on the Astral plane," said the Illusionist, despairing of a better plan.

They flew in a lazy spiral, gradually drawing further and further away from the Scarlet City. An interminable vista of farmlands and woods, plains and fields swung beneath them under the glittering stars and the awful cyclopean glare of the Falling Moon.

The Illusionist sat in the foremost of the bucket-like seats of the kayak, the cowl of his robe drawn up until it covered his face, the better to employ his powers of vision on the Astral.

Around and around they swung, until their spiral had widened to a width of many miles, with the walled city of Chx a clutter of miniature houses far off. No sign of Ganelon Silvermane could be perceived. The Illusionist said nothing, but inwardly he wondered how Ganelon could have come so far, unless he had indeed been mounted on the Bazonga bird. If such proved not to be the case, was it possible that the heroic Construct was dead? At death, the Astral counterpart of the physical body departs for a higher plane of being, to rejoin the Soul, the Spirit and the Zaliph. This is the innermost soul-of-souls, usually resident on the Akashic plane. From the viewpoint of the Akashic, time past, present and future is seen as one continuous palimpsest, he knew. He could not believe that Ganelon Silvermane had been slain. However, every hour their flight continued in an ever-widening circle, it became less likely that the mighty youth could have come so far unaided.

Suddenly, Xarda uttered a stifled shriek. Erigon voiced a startled cry and paddled frantically, as if striving to avert a collision. The magister, whose physical eyes were muffled to insure his higher vision a clearer, unconfused vista, snatched back his cowl and blinked into the wind.

Directly ahead, swinging towards them, an immense flying monster loomed with spread wings black against the argent immensity of the Falling Moon.

# 13.

# *THE OMEGA TRISKELION*

Very early the following morning, Silvermane, accompanied by his escort of metal men, went out on the exercise field and worked himself into a sweat with the pornoí, the yarmak and the war-hammer. He still felt just a trifle sleepy from the narcotics in his wine at dinner the night before, and it was a pleasure to practice with the weapons, stripped to a loin-cloth, under the cool red rays of the aging sun.

Grrff the Tigerman had been working out at the opposite side of the field, practicing with sting-sword, dart-thrower and the traditionally Tigermanic weapon, the ygdraxel. Silvermane had never seen the ygdraxel used before, and studied the Xombolian's technique with claw-tipped, tridentiform billhook appraisingly.

They met, after an hour or so, at the water-butt. Between deep draughts they managed to exchange a few surreptitious morsels of conversation, even though they were under the alert, suspicious eye of Turmus. The Colonel stood near the bleachers, himself conversing with Drng, chief of Zelmarine's Death Dwarves, careful to keep upwind of the bowlegged green monster. He had been imbibing rather heavily of mixed cobra-venom and hydrochloric-acid cocktails the night before, and his breath had to be smelled to be believed.

"Prison scuttlebutt has it the Red Bitch is trying to seduce you; any truth to the rumor?" growled Grrff in low tones, while ostensibly guzzling at the water-pail. Ganelon, who was not too certain what "seduce" meant, made a noncommittal reply. The Tigerman shrugged, took another gulp from the pail, put it down, and began to preen his muzzle and chest-fluff. "None of Grrff's business, eh? Well, maybe so: but you'd better watch your step, big man. Varesco, who nurses a jealous and frustrated passion for the minx, has his eyes on you, and would slay you if he dared. Which he does not. Zelmarine wants to breed a race of supermen wherewith to dominate the world, and needs your,"—he chuckled—"services to that end. She'd skin the old Mind Worshipper alive if she caught him trying to slip some poison into your wine. Keep your eyes peeled when you're alone with Varesco: he knows every sneaky method of assassination and has a hundred ways to kill without leaving clues. The only reason he hasn't put you under the sod already is that he would be the first suspect on the Witch's list if you suddenly turned up your toes and went to Galendil."

Ganelon digested this thoughtfully, while dousing his steaming, naked torso with cold water. "What can we do to escape from this place?" he asked. The cat-yellow eyes of the Tigerman flashed with excited fires.

"Now you're talking! Old Grrff has a few ideas along that line—have you ever heard of the so-called 'Cavern of a Thousand Perils'?"

Ganelon nodded somberly. "I've heard Zelmarine is the last of the Red Amazons, and came hither from Thoph by means of this Cavern. But I don't really understand just what it's supposed to be . . ."

Grrff snorted, blowing water-drops from his whiskers. In his snarling, growly voice he explained: " 'Tis a hyperspatial tube, Grrff's heard, a veritable labyrinth of 'em; connecting different parts o' Gondwane together with other worlds, planes and strata of existence. These hyperspatial tubes collapse space in upon itself; inside one of 'em, a step can take you a hundred leagues, or a thousand, or a quintillion, if you're not careful. Tricksey things, hyperspatial tubes. Nobody knows who built the system, or when, nor even why. Some say the Tensors o' Pluron, others the Fabricators of Dirdanx or the Dional Moralists, or the High Advocats o' Tring or the Ptelian Dynasts, or the Technarchs of Grand Phesion. They've been around since the Age of the Glaspenfells, at least, if not since the Eon of the Blind Philosophers."

Warming to his subject, or perhaps enjoying the chance to display his erudition, the furry Tigerman expanded on the subject. "Some say 'twere the Zealots o' the Black Enigma bent space to make the labyrinth, others say the Mnermite Dissenters, the Nexial Paraphrasts, the Monadic Centralists or the Mysteriarchs of Pesh. At any rate, ol' Grrff, who keeps his ears open and is ever wary, understands the Shai terminus is located somewhere beneath the palace, marked with an Omega Triskelion—"

A sluggish, grating voice spoke suddenly behind them. "Why, you, talk, humans? Go, work, weapons." It sounded like gritty pieces of carborundum being rubbed together in an echo chamber. They turned to see the green dwarfling, Drng, staring at them with dull, suspicious eyes like blood-blisters.

Ganelon did not have a chance, due to Drng's untimely interruption, to ask what an Omega Triskelion was, or why the hyperspatial labyrinth was called "the Cavern of a Thousand Perils". As for the latter question, he thought he could figure it out by himself; it stood to reason that, in a region where a single inaccurate step could carry you across the breadth of Gondwane or to the unknown surface of another planet, the descriptive term "Thousand Perils" might be, if anything, an understatement.

The Omega Triskelion, though, was quite another matter. That afternoon, following a light repast of hot muffins fried in *glick* butter and daubed with dingleberry marmalade, with fricassee of mermaid in calandre sauce, washed down with crystal tumblers of effervescent wine the color of starshine, he sought out the librarium in the Palace of Red Magic. The Enchantress had given him library privileges at his request, to alleviate the boredom of captivity with some light reading. Never much of a reader, the moody giant had browsed through a few odd volumes during the past couple of days.

Now he asked of the librarian, an Automaton whose sentience was attuned to the catalog storage brain, for a volume on signs and symbols. Retiring to an alcove overlooking the Rainbow Fountains, he leafed through Saliche's *Symbolic Imagery* until he found a representation of the sign Grrff had mentioned. It resembled a three-armed swastika composed of open loops with serifs on them. According to Saliche, the curious sign had symbolized open-end infinitism, recorded by the Blind Philosophers of Tring during the Ninth Pastoral Age.* Memorizing the design of the Omega Triskelion, he closed the book and returned it to the metal man.

That evening before moonrise a servant brought to him an invitation to attend Queen Zelmarine at another of those interminable intimate suppers of hers which he found so boring and uncomfortable. The servant also brought him a note from Grrff, which the Tigerman had bribed him to give Silvermane.

In his continuing attempt to figure out Ganelon's sexuality, if any, Varesco had gone back to trying boys to tempt him. This was fortunate, because Grrff could hardly have bribed one of the clanking, empty-headed Automatons.

This particular boy was a languid, lissom lad of twelve or thirteen, as slim, graceful and pretty as a girl. Long blond curls tumbled over his slender shoulders, and he had enormous limpid blue eyes with thick sooty lashes and a soft, pouting mouth. Outside of an abbreviated loincloth of lilac silk, he was naked. Rather

---

* Although why *Blind* Philosophers should use a visual symbol is as much beyond me as it was beyond the redactor of this second book of the Epic, who interpolates a mystified footnote at this same point in the text.

nervously, he slipped Ganelon the note from the Xom-bolian Tigerman. At the same time, he gave him the perfumed invitation from the Red Queen.

His palms had been sweating from sheer anxiety and the ink wherewith Grrff had scrawled the note was smeared, but since the boy wore nothing except the skimpy loincloth and a bit of rouge on a few erog-enous zones, there was nowhere else he could have concealed the note on his person. Ganelon dismissed the child with a somber nod and waited until he had exited before opening Grrff's note. It read as follows:

> *What ho, big man! Prison scuttlebutt says unless you serve the Red Bitch as stud, she'll turn you over to the Ningevite for a Mind Probe. He'll wipe your memory clean and indite a new one, which says you are madly in love with Her Witchery: so watch your step! GRRFF. P.S. The cub bringing you Grrff's note is not as nancy as he looks, runs errands for us sometimes, and can be trusted. His name is Phadia. Keep your whiskers clean! G.*

Ganelon palmed the note and read it while pretending to examine the invitation from the Queen. Then he crushed it in his hand and calmly ate it while munch-ing on a ripe vrique-fruit from the Queen's submarine gardens. He wondered what to do. From what little he knew of Mind Probes, he didn't think he would have any chance of resisting the vindictive Ningevite.

Escape, then, was the only alternative. Ganelon felt embarrassed at the very notion of yielding to the se-duction of the Enchantress. He thought her a very pretty lady, in a slightly overpowering way, but when it came to amatory activity he was completely innocent. It was a matter of actually not knowing just what to do, and with what and where. (For a country boy he was *remarkably* innocent, but his foster-parents had been artisans, not farmers. He never had the opportunity to learn about It from watching the animals.)

Escape, then: but to where, and how? Shai was an island of civilization surrounded by harsh, cindery plains and mountains infested by hordes of Death Dwarves. Overland travel would be hard and hazardous, if not suicidal. He thought of what Grrff had said about the hyperspatial labyrinth called the "Cavern of a Thousand Perils."

On sudden impulse, he touched the gong that summoned the Automatons who guarded him. When the metal man came clanking in, Ganelon gruffly asked for the boy who had just brought him the Queen's invitation. A few moments later the lad entered and came swaying toward him, a tentative smile on his girlish features.

"You want me, lord?" the boy inquired in a husky soprano.

Ganelon cleared his throat with embarrassment and beckoned the boy nearer to him so they could talk without being overheard.

"Grrff the Tigerman says you can be trusted. Your name *is* Phadia, isn't it?" The boy nodded, awaiting his pleasure.

"Are we being watched, Phadia?"

The lad shrugged gracefully, blond curls tumbling over his slim bare shoulders. "I think so, lord. The Lord Varesco is trying to—"

"I *know* what the Lord Varesco is trying to find out," Ganelon grunted uncomfortably. "And I'm really not interested in . . . well, you know."

The boy pouted, then grinned impishly. "Then what *do* you want with me, lord?"

"Information."

"All right, we'll just talk. But, lord, there may be eyes watching us . . . The Lord Varesco will become suspicious if we *just* talk . . . "

"Umm. I guess you're right. Any ideas?"

The lad stretched lazily like a cat, his every movement supple and suggestive. "I'm trained as a dancer, lord. I could dance for you, but stay close enough so we may converse without seeming to do so . . . "

Ganelon nodded, blushing at the picture he would make. The boy laughed at him silently, eyes sparkling with mischief. Slim hips swaying, he went over to a group of hollow crystal wind-chimes hanging in clusters from a mobile and touched them into motion. To the faint chiming music, he began a graceful improvization on an old folkdance of his homeland.

Pretending a rapt fascination, Ganelon watched the slender, swaying figure attentively, blushing furiously all the while. Long bare legs gliding across the carpet, the boy Phadia floated nearer, casting him provocative glances, yet tantalizingly remaining just beyond his reach. If any eyes watched them from a secret spy-hole, they saw more-or-less the sort of thing they would expect to see. They began conversing in low tones, stealthy whisperings.

Ganelon asked the lad if he could move freely about the palace, to which the boy said yes. "Do you know of a room or doorway in the nether regions of the Palace, marked with an Omega Triskelion?"

"I don't know what that is, lord." Ganelon described the symbol. Swaying on his long, supple legs, bare arms undulating to the faint music of the wind-chimes, the boy said he knew of such a portal located in the very bowels of the palace, beneath the wine-cellars.

"But no one can enter, lord: twelve of the metal men guard it night and day."

Pretending that his attention was riveted on the slim, naked boy who danced gracefully before his couch, Ganelon thought swiftly.

"Do you happen to know how the Enchantress controls the metal men?" he asked on an impulse.

The boy cast him a long, sly, coquettish look. Then:

"Yes, I do. Slaves see and hear everything, and nobody ever notices they are around," the boy whispered. Ganelon's pulses jumped.

"How does she turn them off? Tell me?"

The boy drifted nearer. "Only if you promise to take me with you when you escape," the lad whispered.

Ganelon blinked: the child was more clever and quick-thinking than he had guessed. Then he nodded. The boy's eyes shone and he smiled breathlessly.

Then he floated nearer and whispered three words into the ear of Ganelon Silvermane.

# 14.
# THE BOY PHADIA

While her Automatons laid out a cold buffet supper and her maids attired her for the nightly attempt to arouse Ganelon, Zelmarine was attended by Varesco of Ning.

"Have you anything to report, Varesco, or have you come merely to feast your eyes upon that which is un-obtainable?" she asked with sweet cruelty. Averting his eyes from her ripe flesh hastily, the gaunt man flushed a dirty yellow and bowed without speaking.

"Very well, then get on with it."

"Complete failure down the entire spectrum of conceivable perversions," said Varesco in clipped metallic tones. "Save for this evening, when I went back to using boys. Ganelon Silvermane paid scant attention to the youth in question, but then sent for him again, and—"

*"And?"* demanded the Red Queen between stiff lips.

"Nothing much," admitted the Ningevite. "He exchanged a few words with the boy, then apparently asked him to dance for him. The boy danced before him for a time, but the Zermishman made no further advances, merely watching attentively. The boy left, shortly thereafter."

"Did you observe the incident personally?"

"No-o-o," said Varesco reluctantly. The Enchantress glared at him, with brilliant eyes flashing.

"A pity," she said fiercely. "A mental linkage made at that moment, and you could have read the emotional reaction passing through his consciousness, could you not?"

He nodded without speaking.

"Well, what variety of boy was it he asked for?" she inquired. The question was casual, but her jealousy was perfectly obvious in her heaving bosom and glittering eyes. Varesco described the lad.

"White skin, blond hair, long legs, rouge on—"

"Had Ganelon ever seen him before?"

"I doubt it; the child generally serves the prisoners in the main dungeons their luncheon. I instructed that he attend Ganelon Silvermane because he is about thirteen and girlishly pretty. I had previously exposed the Zermishman to boys in the seventeen to twenty-year-old range, with no response whatsoever. Possibly, he prefers them in their early teens—"

"You interrogated the boy, of course?"

"Not I, but my aide, Quang. He questioned the child immediately after Silvermane dismissed him. He said that Silvermane asked his name, age, homeland; learning him to be of Gorombë stock, he asked the boy to perform the traditional 'Moonwillow Leaves' for him. The boy danced with seductive grace; Silvermane watched him attentively, the boy reports, corroborating Quang's own observances, then he bade him leave before the lad could essay a tentative caress."

The Red Enchantress watched her reflection in the huge mirror with cold, hard, cruel eyes while dusky maids dressed her long, darkly-crimson tresses into an elaborate coiffure.

"And what do you deduce from this, Ningevite?" she demanded at length.

Measuring his words carefully, the gaunt man in the narrow tight robes of blinding blue said: "The native dance of that name is performed by Gorombë virgins, just before the mating rituals. Perhaps Ganelon Silvermane as a boy entertained affection for some lad from Gorombë. Brief, unphysical infatuations are typical behavior during adolescence and normal enough," he said with clinical detachment.

"Why this particular boy, I wonder?" mused the Enchantress. "The age factor alone? The color of hair, eyes—?"

"If I might subject the Zermishman to a Mind Probe—"

She said nothing: the subject was one on which they had often had discussions. He adroitly changed the subject.

"—If my hypothesis is correct," he said smoothly, "perhaps this particular boy reminded the Zermishman of some dear little companion of his youth. The experiment, while inconclusive, at least shows more promise than the others." His allusion, of course, was to the parade of men, women, girls, boys and animals which Ganelon had seen in an attempt to find out where his interests lay.

"Have this particular slave attend Ganelon as his servitor from now on," the Red Queen commanded. "Repetition may either dispel the attraction the boy seems to have for him, or lead to something more concrete."

"I hearken and will obey," said Varesco. Then, slyly: "I remain prepared to conduct a depth probe and erasure of the memory centers at your command. I suggest an artificial memory—"

"Useless, you fool, if Ganelon is interested in young boys!" Zelmarine snapped. "Such a diversion of the mating urges lie deep in the instinct-centers of the mind, too deep for you to safely attempt corrective surgery! If necessary, my physicians will extract his spermatozoa and fertilize my ova by artificial insemination. I shall then have his body destroyed!"

The bite of vindictiveness was clear in her deep voice. The Ningevite Mentalist smirked inwardly: artificial insemination, whereby the male fertilizes the female by simple surgical techniques, would have been far easier than this elaborately drawn-out attempt at seduction. But the towering feminine ego of the Queen made it imperative that she succeed in the conquest of her aloof, disinterested superman. She would either conquer Silvermane, or kill him!

Varesco eyed her naked back with hopeless eyes. Whatever happened, his love was futile . . .

After his brief questioning by Varesco's chief spy, the boy Phadia made his way swiftly into the Pueratorium, a huge, barracks-like room he shared with some fifty boys, and entered his own private cubicle. Sponging off his body-rouge and slipping out of his loin-cloth, he slid on a pair of white panties and pulled a light tunic of lavender silk on over his head. The tunic was so short that it barely covered his upper thighs, but it was the best he had. He had long ago sewn a pocket unobtrusively into the lining of it. Now, he secreted some of his best jewelry and a few favorite cosmetics into this hidden pocket and slid his bare feet into gilt slippers.

He did this while keeping his face expressionless, trying not to attract the attention of the other boys who were a catty lot and loved spreading gossip and carrying tales. His heart was pounding with excitement within his breast. The very thought of escaping from this dreary place after all these years was intoxicating. Then he took one last look around the little cubicle which had been his home for so long, to see if he had left anything behind.

All around him, boys between ten and sixteen napped, played games, read, sunbathed, or cuddled with favorite toys, pets or little playmates. Few of them were friends of his, and there were only one or two whom he would particularly miss. On the whole, they were a spoiled, spiteful, effeminate lot and he was weary of them.

He left the huge open room (perhaps for the very last time!) with no regrets or goodbys. Taking seldom-used side-corridors and back-stairs, the lad made his way quickly, unobtrusively to the prison-yard, where captives less coddled than Ganelon Silvermane were sequestered. The few Red Magic sentinels he encountered along the way let him pass without question: the pert, girlishly pretty, good-natured boy was a favorite of theirs. He had long ago established a friendly, first-name relationship with most of them.

The guards stationed at the entrance to the prison-yard also thought nothing of his presence here. They were accustomed to seeing him come and go. Responding to their friendly, flirtatious sally with a coquettish jest, the lad slipped within and soon found Grrff in a sunny corner, playing a half-hearted game of dice with a couple of bored Ixlanders. The big furry fellow looked up with a happy grin as Phadia glided over to him.

"Hah, my pretty cub! Did you—hrmph—do the favor ol' Grrff asked of you?" the Tigerman inquired, with a friendly slap on the lad's bottom. The boy nodded brightly and came near so they could speak confidentially. At Grrff's meaningful glare, the two gloomy Ixlanders hastily went off to continue the game elsewhere.

"The Lord Ganelon asked me where the entrance to the Cavern is," lisped Phadia in his husky soprano. As the Tigerman pricked up his furry, pointed ears, the lad went on to describe the whereabouts of the portal which led into the hyperspatial labyrinth, and to detail Silvermane's rough plan of escape.

"Ho! Good news, for sure," huffed the Karjixian happily. "But when's the day?"

"I don't really know, sir," the boy lisped. "Soon, though. Maybe it will even be today." Then, dropping his thick lashes shyly, the boy whispered softly: "I am to go along, too! He promised."

"Did he now?" rumbled the burly feline amiably. "Well, it pleases ol' Grrff to hear o' that! You don't belong cooped up in here; you've good stuff in you, cub. Better things than paint and perfume, lace and love-notes! Poor lad, it's not your fault, Grrff knows. This is all you've ever known . . . "

The boy smiled tremulously and rose to his feet, bidding the Grrff goodbye. The other grinned, wrinkling up his muzzle, yellow eyes beaming, and gave the lad an affectionate pat on his silk-clad posterior. "Get along with you now, cub; but mind you, keep poor Grrff informed of what's happening!"

The slender boy nodded breathlessly, waved good-bye, and left the prison-yard with a light heart.

On his way from the prison-yard, Phadia ran into a Red Magic legionnaire who was a particular friend of his, a handsome young soldier named Phlay who was fond of little boys and sometimes did small favors for the attractive lad.

"Ah, there, my pretty pet!" the soldier grinned, giving the boy an affectionate pinch. "What's this I hear—your favors are reserved henceforward for the big Zermishman, on orders of the Queen? 'Twill mean heart-break for all your other admirers, I know!"

The boy smiled back. "I'll not neglect my very special friends like you, sergeant," he promised with a provocative flutter of long silken lashes.

"See that you don't," said the other, with a joking pretence of severity. "Anyhow, something tells me your friends will not long languish without their pretty Phadia!"

There was significance to his words. And something went through the boy's slim graceful form, like ice-cold lightning. He shivered slightly.

"What do you mean, sergeant?"

"I mean the Zermish giant had another of his tête-a-tête private suppers with the Queen. He resisted her invitation to more intimate pleasures, which stung her into such a fury that she stunned him with a spell and turned him over to that sly dog, Varesco, on the spot."

The boy swallowed, hardly able to breathe.

"Aye, the big fellow's under the Mind Probe right now, I'll warrant," grinned Phlay. Tousling the lad's blond curls with rough affection, he chucked him under the chin with a fingertip. Then he strolled off about his business, leaving Phadia pale and stiff with horror.

# Book Three

~~~~~~~~~~~~~~~~~~~~~~~~~~~~~~~~~~~~~~~~

# *THE GRANDFATHER OF ALL DRAGONS*

*The Scene:* Shai, and the Dungeons Thereof; The Cavern of a Thousand Perils; The Halfworld of Faerie; Dzimdazoul's Deep.

*New Characters:* Hawkmen, Merfolk, Gnomes, and the Denizens of several Worlds and Planes; The Oldest of All Dragons, a Kindly Cockatrice, and a Lovesick Lady Sphinx.

# 15.
# MEETING IN THE MOUNTAINS

Erigon yelled, Xarda shrieked, the Illusionist swore! To their left, a cliffy wall of mountains blocked the world away: before them the winged monster loomed, a weird black mass etched with moonsilver.

With remarkable presence of mind, Prince Erigon kicked the pedals. Istrobian's flying kayak skidded around in a tight half-circle, narrowly missing the monster, which hovered motionlessly on out-stretched wings.

"It's not moving!" and "It's the Bazonga!" exlaimed Sarda and the Illusionist, in virtually the same breath. They blinked and looked again. It was indeed the dear Bird! She floated listlessly, drifting a little in the thrust and ebb of the air-currents. Her lens-eyes were dull and lifeless, her hinged back gaped open. The old magician hailed her, but the ungainly sentient vehicle made no response.

"Look at the dent in her crest," said the girl knight breathlessly. "Just in front of her top-knot! I do believe she has done herself an injury. Could she have flown into the cliff for some reason?"

The old magician said: "It is not at all unlikely, my child. These are the Vanishing Mountains, which form the border between the Country of the Death Dwarves and Chx, unless my sense of geography fails me."

"You said *Vanishing* Mountains?" repeated the Prince of Valardus. "A curious term."

"But singularly apt in this instance," said the Illusionist. "Sometimes they are here and at other times they are not. Please do not ask me to explain it all now! I must get aboard the dear Bird and explore the extent of her injuries. Dear me, I will never forgive myself is she has . . . can you bring the kayak closer to her flank and hold the craft steady while I climb into the cockpit?"

"I guess so," said Erigon dubiously. He fiddled with the pedals; Istrobian's flying kayak inched closer to the lifeless bronze shape until it nuzzled her sides. The magician gingerly stood up and fumbled about in order to get a firm grip on the edge of the Bazonga's cockpit. Xarda watched, her green eyes bright with nervousness.

"Oh, magister, let me! I am young and agile—"

"But completely untutored in crystalloid lifeforms," he said curtly. "You wouldn't know what to look for. No talking now!" The kayak wobbled drunkenly as the old magician climbed from it into the bronze vehicle. When the magician was safely ensconced in the cockpit Erigon released, with a whoosh of relief, the breath he had been holding.

"I shall have to climb out on her neck to examine her skullcase," the Illusionist announced. "If she did indeed run into the mountain wall, the collision may have jarred a few of her electrodes loose, or broken a connection." Xarda bit her lip and gripped Prince Erigon's hand tightly as the old man got out on the neck of the Bazonga, to sit astride it as one sits on a treebranch. Reaching forward, he grasped the Bird's bronze top-knot and pulled himself up the neck. The Bazonga bobbed as his weight shifted, and her beak dipped earthwards. Fumblingly he snapped the catches, opened her skull-case, and peered within.

The brilliance of the Falling Moon was nearly as bright as a flashlight would have been. A moment or two later, he called back to them that the sentient crystalloid which served as the creature's brain seemed not to have been harmed, nestled snugly in its velvet padding, but three of the copper wire electrodes which connected the crystal brain to the flying and sensory apparatus were indeed out of their sockets. Probing within the skull cavity, and cursing under his breath as he tried to recall the color code with which the proper terminal connections had originally been marked, he carefully inserted the electrodes one by one.

It seemed to take forever. When it was over and the mood of suspense broke, only then did the girl knight of Jemmerdy realize she had been holding onto Prince Erigon's hand for dear life. She snatched her hand away, crimsoning with embarrassment: the engaging young Valardian, however, seemed to have rather enjoyed their fleeting moment of closeness. He grinned at her; she flashed him a disdainful glance and looked away, furious at her momentary display of unfeminine weakness.

It took a few minutes for the dear Bird to recover herself. When she was herself again, she was surprised and pleased to see them again and shyly made the Prince's acquaintance. Privately, she too thought him remarkably good-looking—for a True Man, that is.

"It was like taking a little nap," the garrulous Bird marveled to herself. "Everything was so cozy and dreamy again—just like being snugly nested back in the bowels of Old Earth (if I may be forgiven so unladylike a phrase!), with all my brother and sister crystalloids beside me, warm and snuggy in the pre-Diluvian strata. Now I know what you human beings experience when you 'go to sleep', as you so quaintly term it! Why, it's rather pleasant and comfy, after all . . ."

The magister, seated stiffly in the cockpit once again, ground his teeth together and swore under his breath by the Twelfth Mystery of Pesh, the Black Vortex, and the Magneto-gravitic Nexus.

"If you are *quite* done," he snapped, "we are more than a little concerned to find out just what has been happening! How did you get here? What have you done with Ganelon Silvermane?"

"Oh, pish-tush, you old fussbudget," sang the Bird carelessly. "Why, he's right back there, where I left him only a moment before!" With a casual flip of her wing, she indicated an area of broken slabs on the first slopes of the Vanishing Mountains.

"D-do you mean *there* . . . where all the Death Dwarf corpses are?" asked Xarda fearfully. The Bird admitted that was where she had deposited the young giant, before flying back to fetch to safety the rest of them.

"But I see you have managed ro rescue yourselves! *And* this nice young Prince," she added in a coyly flirtatious manner, which the old magician found faintly sickening. For the nine-hundredth time, he wondered why "that senile old idiot"* had seen fit to give his creation the psychic orientation of a talkative old aunt, when he had electrically educated the intelligent crystalloid.

They brought the kayak and the Bazonga bird down to the surface; Erigon hopped out to investigate the situation at first hand. He returned a while later to say that Ganelon's corpse was not to be seen, but that the evidence suggested the giant had fought a terrific battle against the Death Dwarves, slaying many.

"Could he have wandered off, injured perhaps, or dazed?" inquired the old magician. Prince Erigon shook his head unhappily.

"I really don't believe so," he said regretfully. "I would say the surviving Dwarves finally overpowered him and carried him off to their lairs. This seems to be what happened, from the fact that the dwarf corpses have been plundered of their weapons, which Ganelon Silvermane would not have done. He might have armed himself with a sword, club, axe or two, but not a dozen or more."

The knightrix of Jemmerdy swallowed a painful lump and measured the moonlit distances with grimly resolute eyes.

"If he's captive somewhere in Dwarfland, then we

---

* Meaning Miomivir Chastovix, the wizard who built the Bazonga.

must go after him," she said determinedly. "By my halidom, 'tis the very least we owe the great lout!"

The Illusionist agreed anxiously: he had become very fond of the youthful Construct by now, and would have deeply regretted losing him. They took to the air again, Xarda and Erigon in the flying kayak and the old magician riding in the Bazonga's cockpit. The night was half done; by dawn they had traversed the Country of the Death Dwarves from north to south, from east to west. Nowhere, in all this realm of sterile mountains and bleakly barren plains, had the Illusionist managed to detect the distinctive spectrum of Ganelon's Auric radiation.

"Isn't it true that the little abominations lair in caverns and holes in the ground?" asked Xarda when the search had ended at dawn, in failure. The Illusionist nodded wearily.

"Quite true, but solid matter is completely transparent on the Astral plane. Ganelon's Aura would be perfectly visible to Third Eye vision, even were he penned in subterranean regions. No, we shall have to give up on Dwarf country."

"What then?" inquired Erigon, trying unsuccessfully to stifle a yawn.

"The Land of Red Magic," said the Illusionist. "The little monsters who attacked Ganelon must have come from those tribes over which the Red Enchantress has gained dominance."

"That means we must begin our search for the boy all over again, in the next kingdom!" groaned the knightrix. "And I can hardly keep my eyes open, after so busy and eventful a night."

"Well, we can safely nap while en route," said the magician. "We do require sleep, for we must be sharp, alert and have all our wits about us when we confront Zelmarine in the very fortress of her power . . ."

"How can we do that, though?" countered Prince Erigon. "You can safely snooze in your quaint vehicle, who flies herself . . . but Istrobian's flying kayak is a bird of a different feather, if you will permit me the lame jest."

"Tether the kayak to the Bird's tail with the sentient rope, then join us in the cockpit for a snooze," suggested the Illusionist, practically. "Our search has ended here at the westernmost corner of Dwarfland, facing on the Voormish desert; we have, I should say, three or four hours of flight before reaching the vicinity of Shai, the Red Queen's capitol. Luckily, the dear Bird requires no rest, and can fly herself while we yield to the demands of nature."

The plan made excellent sense. By this time, Prince Erigon was falling asleep. Securing the kayak to the peacock tail of the Bazonga, he clambered into the rear seat of the cockpit, snuggled down in his cloak, and fell sound asleep in an instant. Xarda and the old magician were not far behind him, entering the embrace of Morpheus.

The Bazonga regarded them fondly in her rear-vision mirror; then, flying smoothly so as not to jolt her sleeping passengers into wakefulness, she cruised up into the middle air and pointed her beak in the direction of the Land of Red Magic.

Or in what she *thought* was the direction, that is.

For in all her circlings and searchings, the poor Bird had become turned about, so she was headed directly north.

The Land of Red Magic, of course, lay due east. But the Bazonga had flown over Horx and eastern Ixland and was well beyond Yombok, before she had the slightest inkling of the fact that she was flying in exactly the wrong direction.

# 16.
# *THE MIND-PROBE*

Stripped and bound to the gleaming metal table under strong lights, Ganelon Silvermane lay helpless. Over him brooded the hunched form of the Mentalist, Varesco, his fierce blue robes exchanged for laboratory whites. Atop the bare skull of the Mind Worshipper sat a peculiar helmet of glittering metal parts, connected by flashing glassy tubes and winking bulbs, a device which augmented and channeled the focused mental power of the wearer.

Already, the Ningevite had inserted his mentality into the surface layers of the giant's sleeping mind. He watched, if that's the word I want, the ebb and flicker of surface thoughts. These were chiefly concerned with people whom Varesco did not know—with names like "master", "Xarda" and "the Bird." Riffling through these thoughts, the residue left by a suddenly anaesthetized consciousness, the Mind Worshipper found nothing of particular interest. He began to probe deeper.

To the unique telepathic sense of the Mentalist, the mind of a being such as Ganelon Silvermane resembles a sphere composed of innumerable layers. Beneath the surface flow of thoughts and memories lie the centers of consciousness and of will, character and personality. Within these, yet deeper down, lies the Unconscious itself, the home of powerful instinctive drives and hungers. Deeper yet, at the very core of the human mind, are found the inner-most citadels of identity where lie vast, seldom-tapped reservoirs of dormant strengths, vitalities, and the secret recesses of the soul.

107

Varesco hated the giant with every iota of his warped and withered self. Hated him for being young, strong and handsome, in a craggy, heavy-jawed way (handsomer than sallow, lank-jawed Varesco, at any rate!); hated him for being brave and gallant, generous, faithful and good. In brief, for being everything that Varesco was not, had never been, and never would be. This hatred was deep and instinctive: Varesco himself was conscious only that he resented the young giant for catching the eye of Zelmarine, for whom the Mentalist had long ago conceived a helpless, overwhelming passion.

Sliding down the centers of consciousness, Varesco inserted tendrils of thought deep into the centers of Ganelon's being. It was now completely within his power to destroy the youth he loathed with a hatred that was completely visceral. One savage slashing of those tendrils, and Silvermane would be reduced to a slobbering cretin, a mindless vegetable hulk, or a roaring maniac. A deeper thrust, to sever the connections of the soul, and the giant would be a cooling, lifeless cadaver.

But Varesco was not insane, despite his cruelty and rabid fervors. He was, in truth, very sane; sane enough to realize that should he once give way to the urge to rip and destroy the mind of Silvermane, his own death would soon follow. The Enchantress desired Silvermane with every particle of her being. She would not hesitate to destroy Varesco, should he murder the object of her passion.

Entering the region of the instinctive drives, Varesco traced circuits and nodes with practiced skill. Silvermane's sexuality, he discovered, did not lie in the dominion of the greater or lesser perversions. It was, quite simply, dormant. At the sexual level, Silvermane was less than twelve years old—prepubescent—although on the physical level he was fully mature, and his emotional and intellectual growth was not far behind.

Below the centers of instinct, Varesco was surprised to discover nine centers previously unmapped by the

Mentalists of Ning. He had no idea of their role in the makeup of the giant: they were mysterious, unheard-of. Curious as to their purpose, he inserted a probe. The nodes and circuits in this deep region were intensely peculiar; he could trace them with ease, but knew not what impulses they were designed to carry.

He probed on, increasingly enthralled.

Phadia knew where the mind laboratory was located, of course, as he knew every nook and cranny of the palace of red glass. The bright, inquisitive boy had long ago explored the palace from top to bottom on one pretext or another, reasoning that the more he knew of his captors and this place, the better he would be prepared for the moment when a chance to strike for escape and freedom came. He had always known it would someday come, and had long prepared himself for it.

He went to Varesco's suite simply because he could think of nothing else to do. If discovered, he could always pretend to be carrying a message, or could wheedle his way past the friendly, indulgent guards who had long since made a pet of him. He was a familiar fixture in the palace of Red Magic, knew all of the palace guards by first name and built a relationship of joking flirtation with most of them. He trusted this to get him out of trouble, should he be caught.

Varesco's suite was never locked. Few doors in the Palace of Red Magic were ever locked, because Zelmarine was always suspicious of what might be brewing behind locked doors, and her courtiers quickly learned to disarm her suspicions early on. Thus, the boy found it easy to steal within, gliding stealthily from room to darkened room, until he entered the laboratory itself.

The room was scrupulously clean and brilliantly lit by tall standards, which supported fiercely luminous globes. The walls and floor were covered with tiles, immaculately white. Long marble benches supported ranks of flasks, trays of stoppered tubes, and other chemical apparatus. Banks of curious instruments loomed in the corners of the room: meters whirled, dials ticked, lights flickered on and off. The remnants of a forgotten age of science lingered, it would seem, among the savants of Ning.

Directly in the center of the room, Ganelon Silvermane lay strapped to a reclining table, his nude bronze torso gleaming with perspiration. Over him, with his back turned to the door where Phadia lurked, Varesco stood bending over the giant. His peculiar helm caught the boy's fascinated eye. Obviously, the Mind Probe was in progress. Phadia, his heart hammering against the cage of his ribs, crept forward on furtive feet.

He wondered if he were in time . . .

Or too late?

Clenching his teeth, the boy glided across the laboratory. For a weapon, he dug into the pocket sewn on the inner lining of his tunic and found a long steel hairpin which ended in a cluster of twinkling gems.

Something alerted Varesco, perhaps the scrape of sandal-leather against the tiles. He started to straighten up, but it was too late. Phadia struck like a darting serpent, and the steel needle entered the nape of his neck and transfixed his brain.

Ganelon blinked slowly awake to find slender arms wound around his neck and a weeping boy clinging to his chest, cheek pillowed upon his heart. For a moment the bronze giant did not know where he was; then, turning his head about, he saw Varesco lying on his back in a pool of blood. The sour, sallow face, usually tight and thin-lipped, was for once relaxed and at peace.

"It's all right, Phadia," said Ganelon gently. "It's all over now."

The boy raised his head and looked at Ganelon, lips trembling with astonishment. He wiped his tear-stained cheeks and rubbed his eyes. "I thought you were . . . dead!"

Ganelon grinned, sat up, snapping his bonds as if

they were bits of rotten twine. "Outside of a skull-splitting headache," he said, "I am unharmed."

He got off the table, reached over and brushed the long blond curls back from the boy's face, tousling his hair affectionately. He said nothing.

"Did I . . . did I do right?" the boy asked.

He nodded somberly. "You did just fine. Where do they keep Grrff?"

Grrff did not seem particularly surprised to see the big bronze man and the slender boy. He grinned, wrinkling up his muzzle, yellow eyes glistening with lively spirits. While Ganelon broke his fetters with a twist of his mighty hands, the Tigerman hugged the boy till he gasped. Then he turned to clap Ganelon's bare shoulder with one huge paw.

"Ho, big man!" he roared. "How many guards did you have to kill to get down here to set Grrff free?"

"Five or six," grunted Silvermane, hefting a severely dented copper bar. "C'mon, the whole palace is on our heels."

"Which way?"

"The crypts beneath the dungeons. This way!"

They ran down a spiral staircase, feet pounding, the boy breathlessly pattering after them. It was a remarkable sight: the huge, burly-shouldered, furry Tigerman with his lashing tail, the slim effeminate boy in the skimpy abbreviated lavender silk tunic, his long bare legs slender and girlish, and—Silvermane, his bronze hide gleaming, as bare as the day he was born.

"Hah!" snorted the Tigerman. "I see time was of the essence." He winked at Ganelon's bare hide. The silver-haired giant flushed.

"No time to look for my harness," he grunted unhappily. "Quang stuck his nose in the door and ran off squeaking to sound the alarm. So I escaped like this!"

"How do we get past the metal men?" huffed Grrff a few moments later.

"We turn them off," said Ganelon. "Phadia told me how."

The door loomed before them, a slab of crimson metal set flush with the stone wall. The Omega Triskelion was blazoned huge across the double leaves of the portal, black enamel on scarlet metal.

Before the door, metal men were ranked. Motionless as so many empty suits of armor they stood, their arms thrust out before them, terminating in hooks, claws, scythes, power drills, hammers and axes. As the three escapees came pelting down the stair towards them, suddenly they became animate, clanking to attack position. The drill-arms started up with a whirring sound.

"If you know how to do it, you'd better do it now," rumbled Grrff, eyeing the Automatons warily.

Ganelon stepped forward until the hook-arm of the foremost Automaton almost touched his naked chest.

*"Turn yourselves off!"* he roared.

The metal men collapsed on all sides, leg-joints clattering, like a cast of wooden puppets whose strings are simultaneously cut. Snatching up Phadia in his arms, Ganelon wove through the mound of lifeless metal, grasped the handle of the door and jerked. It came open with a groan of rusty metal, revealing a yawning blackness.

"Does anybody know where we're going?" asked Grrff, as they lingered for a moment at the mouth of the Cavern.

"Does anybody care?" grunted Ganelon, as he stepped across the threshold—

# 17.

# THE CAVERN OF
# A THOUSAND
# PERILS

The moment they stepped across the threshold, the doorway dwindled and vanished far behind them. Huddled against Ganelon's breast, the boy gasped and cowered.

They had taken one step only. Since the hyperspatial tube collapsed space in upon itself, that one step might have been the equivalent of a hundred miles, or a thousand. Or a million! It was enormously risky: they had no idea of where they were, or of where the next step might take them. To the Isles of Quadquoph, or the far side of the Moon, or Beta Draconis! Presumably, when powerful and cunning sorcerors like the Illusionist or Zelmarine used the labyrinth, they had some knowledge of how to get to where they wanted to be.

Ganelon stood motionless, straining every nerve. Beneath his bare soles he felt gritty cavern floor, naked stone, wet and sandy. His nostrils, however, reported the heady odor of jungle orchids and decaying leaves, while the wind that blew upon his nakedness was sharp dry and chill as Arctic winds. He could see nothing at all: impenetrable blackness veiled his sight.

"I'm af-f-fraid!" the boy whimpered, burying his face in against Ganelon's breast.

"Hush!" said the giant fondly. "Don't you think we all are? Grrff!"

"Right beside you, big man," said that worthy, "and beginning to wish he had stayed behind to take his chances with the Red Magic legionnaires."

"We'd better go carefully, from here on in," counseled the giant. "Half a step difference between us could separate us by thousands of miles. Hold onto me and take a step when I do." The big furry paw fastened itself to his upper arm. "Together now! One—*big*—step—"

Seawater, bluely-green, closed around them. Instinctively, all three hyperspatial travelers held their breaths. Pale sand squelched underfoot, strewn with glimmering moony pearls and human skulls, mossy with sea-growths. In the distance the elfin-slim coral towers of a marine city leaned against the tides, flashing with huge gems. Mounted on enormous, goggle-eyed sea-horses, a troop of sea-folk sped towards them, waving tridents angrily. They were male and female, naked with green hair like seaweed floating out behind them; minute, pearly scales glittered with highlights on smooth thigh, breast, shoulders.

They took another big step—

Jagged peaks zoomed above them, standing against wind-torn cloud-wracks like tall chimneys. Each was crowned with a huge nest. Scrawny female figures with flying hair and beaked faces shrieked and gobbled down at them, waving long skinny arms which terminated in hooked claws. A loud halloo came down the wind: gaunt man-birds, black wings spread, came soaring down, angry eyes flashing, beaks snapping. They staggered to keep their footing in the winds which streamed about them, drying the sea-bottom wetness in moments. Grrff tried to say something but the wind snatched his words away.

They took another wide step—

Forest greenery closed in about them, leaves dark green and silvery where floods of moonlight poured through ragged branches. Gnarled, ancient trees grew all about; green aisles ran in all directions, thick with red and yellow mushrooms. Small, stunted figures ran squeaking to hide behind knotted roots and to peer out at the strangers. The gnomes had huge noses, tiny squinting eyes, and thick, bedraggled beards like moss. Some puffed on huge meerschaum pipes, others clutched quaint musical instruments they had been tootling on mere moments before. They squeaked and peered, waving tiny fists in a threatening manner. Suddenly hooves drummed through the forest still: a huge manlike figure, but faceless, black as tarnished silver, crowned with slender needles of ice, rode through the underbrush to rein before them. He was mounted upon a milk-white Unicorn whose arched, noble neck, blazing ruby eyes and long, spiral-fluted horn of purest gold flashed before them like something from a fantastic dream. The black-silver man with no face gestured towards them with a long sceptre of crystal or ice.

They took another step—

Flames roared up, gold and crimson. Hot, scorching winds smote them, stinking of sulphur and brimstone. Beneath their feet, stone glowed hotly, threaded with sluggish, crawling rivulets of bubbling lava. Huge, lumpish figures rose amid the seething flames, peering out at them with astonishment, heavy jaws hanging wide, blunt tusks gleaming. The fire-ogres had armored skins like crocodiles, horns grew at brow and temple, elbow, knee and shoulder. Their heavy, splay-feet were those of monstrous lizards. One ogre burst bellowing through the curtain of flames, whirling a whistling club around his head broken from a stalagmite. He howled, gushing steam from his mouth, and loped towards them.

They took another step—

Parched and dry, the desert sands stretched from horizon to horizon under seven burning suns of metallic indigo, canary yellow, olive green, grayish purple, and three other colors for which the dazed, bewildered

travellers had no names. Stone colossi marched across
the desert, hundred-foot-high figures of manlike marble, but headless, who walked with a grating, gritty
sound of stone rubbing against stone. From whence
they came and to what unthinkable destination the
stone monsters were bound was equally unknown. With
each step the ponderous giants took, the desert
drummed and sand jumped. A black shadow, edged
with penumbra of seven colors, fell over them. They
stared up wildly to see a vast stone foot coming down—
and took another step themselves.

They stood on ice, slick as glass. Above the immense
glacier, northern lights flickered, forming an undulating, ghostly luminous banner. Frost sprinkled them
from head to foot: their three breaths steamed before
them like white plumes. A distant yelping echoed across
the plain of ice. In a moment, a slithering horde of
white reptiles with vicious red eyes and long alligator
tails came swarming into view around icy pinnacles of
glimmering green. The ice-dwelling reptiles were yer-
xels; Ganelon had fought them before on Mount Droom
so he knew that, wherever they were, at least they were
back to Gondwane. Hissing like so many tea-kettles,
the white lizards cames squirming towards them, claws
skittering on the ice.

They took another step—

Dim green gloom closed about them now; a stone roof
soared far above, supported by pillars that looked like
stalagmites, and probably were. The cavern was unthinkably immense, cool and dim and echoing. But, at
least, it seemed uninhabited. Still holding Phadia cuddled against his breast, Ganelon staggered. The sudden
transitions from hot to cold, wet to dry, left him numb
and feeling somehow pummeled.

They peered about them, cautiously. Nearby a great
mound of boulders like a rocky hill loomed up,
dim and glittering with lots of sharp rocky ridges. Beyond arched the cavern wall, gleaming with eerie phos-

phorescence. Underfoot, gems crunched. At first the three mistook them for pebbles, but then Grrff stopped, bent down, scooped up a pawful and let them trickle through his digits. A glinting cataract of chatoyants, beryls, garnets, amethysts and alexandrites.

"A duke's ransom!" he huffed, eyes following the dazzling stream.

Ganelon wearily set the boy down, cautioning him not to stray. Phadia knelt and gathered up a handful of coins. They were old and tarnished—coins of copper, silver, gold, electrum, platinum, and metals blue, green, black, for which he had no name. Some were round, others square or oval; some bore portraits either profile or full-face; the inscriptions were in languages he could not read. The floor of the cavern was completely covered with coins and gems, as far as the eye could reach. And it was an awfully large cavern.

Ganelon turned and looked behind him. Their last step had carried them through a stone archway whose keystone bore the Omega Triskelion symbol. They were out of the labyrinth and safe for a while, it seemed.

He sat down on a rounded boulder, smooth with lichens, to catch his breath.

"I guess we're safe here," he said moodily. Something had happened to him under the Mind Probe, but the whirl of events had moved so swiftly that he had not yet had leisure time to evaluate it.

"Hmph! But where is *here?*" gruffed the Tigerman, looking about him skeptically.

Stretched out on his tummy, kicking his heels in the air, small chin resting on folded hands, Phadia peered drowsily into the glitter of heaped gems. Their lights sent a flicker of enchantment across his pretty, girlish face.

"Maybe this is dragon treasure," he suggested dreamily, "and we're in a dragon's cave!"

Grrff snorted, twitching his whiskers.

"Nonsense, cub! Fairy-tale-stuff! There are no dragons left in Gondwane . . . "

*This isn't Gondwane,* said a huge voice, making them all jump. It was a deep, grumbly voice with a lot of hissing in it: sort of the kind of voice thunder might make if it tried to hiss at the same time. None of them had ever heard a voice remotely like it before, and the alarming thing was they could not see whom it was that had spoken.

Then the big, dim, sharply-ridged hill in front of them opened one huge eye, like a bright green full moon and winked at them!

*This is a Dragon's cave,* said the voice again. And this time they saw that it did come from the hill. Only it wasn't a hill, it was—

*And I'm the dragon,* said the Dragon.

# 18.
# THE OLDEST ONE

Phadia jumped to his feet and tried to stuff the fingers of both hands into his mouth, eyes wide and unbelieving. Ganelon hefted the bent copper bar wherewith he had fought his way from Varesco's laboratory to the prison-yard, and wished for his Silver Sword. And, as for Grrff, the burly Tigerman growled deep in his chest, hackles rising on his nape, razory black claws bared, eyes glowing sulphurously through the dim greenish gloom.

The craggy hill in front of them opened a second great moon-eye with which to observe them interestedly. The monster was big as a house, big as a blockfull of houses, but it did not seem to be interested in dinner; at least, not at the moment. Some gigantic prehistoric monster, some huge lizard, some sentient saurian strayed here from Earth's forgotten prime? Whatever it was, they had little hopes of fighting it.

*Manlings, here in my lair?* it murmured in that hissy, thunderthroated voice. *How wondrous strange! Has been a thousand ages, aye, and more, since last Dzimdazoul had manlings as his guests . . . put up thy copper club, Silverhair! Dzimdazoul hath ever been that friendly with thy kind, to win him place within thy legendry.*

They began to relax, joint by joint, nerve by nerve. Something behind or underneath the words themselves stole fright from them, bit by bit. They began to stare at the great Dragon, open-mouthed with amazed and wide-eyed wonderment, as the enormous friendly crea-

119

ture regarded them with luminous, unwinking, philo-
sophical and faintly humorous gaze.

They could see Dzimdazoul more clearly now, their
eyes having adjusted to the dim green gloom. He had a
broad head with prominent brow-ridges that curved
above the great moon-like eyes, and a long, wrinkled,
scaly snout with large nostrils from which exhaled a
whiff of sulphurous steam as he breathed. When he
grinned, as he did in a manner meant to be friendly,
he exposed fangs longer than a man's arms. The size
of him, the scaly length, was preposterous—mythical!

The dragonish breed had long-since vanished from
Gondwane by their age, lingering only in legend and
in a few remnants of the race, dwarfed and mute,
which lurked in crypts and caverns much like this one.
But this was one of the Old Dragons, the great dragons
of the Prime, and huger than any living thing had
any right to be.

Curiously enough, it was little Phadia who was the
first to lose his fear of Dzimdazoul. Smiling with shy
wonder, he crept forward and seated himself timidly
on one of the Dragon's paws which were stretched out
before him. The Dragon regarded the boy with friendly
inquisitiveness, cocking his great head first on one side,
then the other, like some enormous dog.

*A man-child, is it?* he hissed affably.

"Yes, sir," said the boy in a very small voice. The
Dragon chuckled—an unnerving sound like several ava-
lanches rumbling down a very tall mountain.

*Hath more courage, the lad, than either of yon
great burly louts,* Dzimdazoul chuckled. *Or be it
common-sense? Aye, you've nought to fear from old
Dzimdazoul, little men! I was a friend to your kind
when your first ancestors came furtively out of the
forests; clad in hair, were ye then, not unlike yonder
cat-man there, with wee small tails, and ye chattered
like the monkeys ye had been, not long before.*

Ganelon blinked. His master had taught him about
the theory of evolution, so he had some notion of the
age of the Earth and of the human race. What the

great reptile had said in its lazy, hissing rumble was purely incredible.

"Are you . . . can you be . . . *that* old, great one?" he asked dazedly. The Dragon grinned, wrinkling his leathery old snout. Then his green moon-eyes grew dreamy, as if he looked back down the long interminable ages since Creation.

*I am the First Dragon*, he said sleepily; *I am the Old One, the oldest of the Old Things . . . the Demiurge made me first, after the Earth itself; 'twas Deos-Ptah, or somesuch like that, was his name . . . Ialdabaoth came later, then all the other Gods who have ruled Old Earth from my time to thine. Do Zul and Rashemba rule thy world still, or be it young Galendil now? . . . I have slept the last million years away, here in mine cozy Deep, and be somewhat out of touch with Time! Ah, well, no matter . . .*

*Can I in truth be as old as that, you ask, Silverhair? . . . I am the oldest, the most ancient, of all living things. I remember the wars of Troy and the drowning of Atlantis. I watched the little brown men as they built the pyramids . . . I knew Aristotle and Charlemagne, and once I saw Alexander from a distance, riding down the long, long road to India. Already was I past the middle of my youth when the first nomad hunters strayed into the uncharted wilderness that was prehistoric Europe; and when I was very, very young, I saw Father Adam driven out of Paradise by a stern and beautiful angel with a sword of flame! Oh, I am very old; I am older than the Moon; I am nearly as old as Old Earth itself . . . and I am older by far than the race of man. I have forgotten more things than man has ever learned, because I am older than man. I remember things even the mountains have forgot.*

Very little of what the Old Dragon said meant anything to any of them, for the realms and kings of Earth's youth had long since faded from man's memory, before ever Gondwane was formed out of the coming-together of the drifting continents. But Ganelon understood a little of it, just enough to feel awe. He spoke up and asked the Dragon just how old he was.

The great eyes twinkled at him humorously.

*I really do not know! I have forgotten long ago; but very much older than you would think reasonable. I remember Julius Caesar and Hannibal, and I once saw Semiramis riding in a procession full of dancing girls and feather-fans. I can remember what Salisbury Plain looked like before Stonehenge. I watched the fall of Babylon and the burning of Persepolis, and I once discussed the circumference of the world with Ptolemy. I remember the first ship and the first city. I think I can remember the discovery of fire, but I'm not quite certain whether it was a caveman named Og who discovered it, or another named Ak; Og had blue eyes and yellow hair, as I recall; he was probably a Cro-Magnon......*

The voice of the Old Dragon lulled them into a dreamy daze; curled up on Dzimdazoul's paw, Phadia was fast asleep, his thumb tucked into his mouth, worn out from the excitements of the day. Ganelon and Grrff sat on the cavern floor, listening as the Old Dragon talked of things long ago and far away, another world, another age. Grrff understood little of what the great creature said, but listened anyway, enthralled.

*I remember before the poles changed; I remember Ultima Thule. And I knew Hercules, or rather, one of the forty wandering heroes whose various exploits got mixed up in the story of Hercules. I saw the Crusades; I knew Roland, yes, and Oliver; I watched the Ice Age come and go.......I saw the first dog, while the Northern Lights glimmered overhead and the ice lay deep across Europe.*

*I used to spend my winters in the palace of Prester John. I saw the Huns come riding out of Asia, and the Mongols, and the Turks; the Tartars, too. I remember the death of the last mastodon and of the last wooly mammoth.*

*And I remember Siegfried.*

"How is it, Grandfather, that you have lived so long?" asked Ganelon sleepily.

*I was the first living thing which the Demiurge made, after the creation of the world itself—Theos-Pater, was that his name?—I think he loved me for that I was his first; at any rate, he let me live longer than any other thing. In the Beginning there were only Behemoth and Leviathan and I. Leviathan lived in the sea; Behemoth roamed the great plains; and I resided in the caverns underneath the world.......they died young, my mighty brothers. There was not enough in the world for them to eat, so Dyaus-Ptah, or whatever his name was, took their lives away from them. But I was his first living creature, and he could not bear to take my life back; so he arranged it that I fed only on gems and precious minerals, whereof the world hath a great plenty......then, I think, he just forgot about me, and Ialdabaoth never knew I was even there . . . later on, of course, I found my way Here.*

"Where is 'here'?" murmured Silvermane, sleepily. "This isn't Gondwane, is it?" The Old Dragon shook his heavy head ponderously.

*This is the Halfworld: some call it Faërie. 'Tis a midregion outside of the world, yet part of it in a certain sense. And connected with many other worlds as well. Here death cannot ever come, because we are outside of Time and beyond the reach of Change. Here Arthur sleeps, and Charlemagne and Barbarossa, and Ogier; and here Merlin dreams the world away, lonely in Brociliande—*

The deep, hissing, thunderous voice slowed to a halt. The Old Dragon peered down at them with huge, curious, wise eyes; they were asleep, all three. The Tigerman slept on his back, his paws lifted before his furry chest. He snored, a kind of purring sound.

*Sleep, now, little ones . . . I had forgotten how easily you manlings weary . . . sleep! No harm can come to you here, and I will watch over your rest,* said the Old Dragon.

# 19.

# ON THE PURPLE PLAIN

Aboard the Bazonga the Illusionist and his party were also fast asleep, worn out from the long night's travels and adventures. Not daring to disturb the slumbering humans, the Bird flew on into the north, although by now the poor befuddled creature was beginning to suspect that she was doing something wrong.

Poy was behind them, and Cham. The Sea of Glass glimmered beneath her keel, that vast expanse of sand which once had been a desert or the bottom of a vanished sea, before an exploding contraterrene meteorite had fused it to one sparkling flatness of crystal. The Bird circled low, peering down curiously, admiring her reflection in it.

The Sun came up; still the same Sun of our own day, but older now, redder and cooler, a dimming star-candle, guttering towards extinction. A billion years, more or less, and Old Earth's last and final dawn would break . . .

It was the sunlight in his eyes that roused the old magician from his sleep. He woke, and stretched, and scratched himself and spat over the side. He looked around him, rheumy-eyed, wishing he were back in his own soft bed at Nerelon, with Fryx to bring him his morning cocoa—

Beneath them an illimitable plain of thick purple grasses rolled to the horizon.

He jumped, cursed in three extinct languages and one

ultra-terrestrial one, and clutching the edge of the cockpit, stared down with horror.

The Bird winked at him in her rear-vision mirror.

" 'Awake! for morning in the—' "

"You mechanistic imbecile! You moronic vehicle, you—! You sub-cretinous contraption—*what, have, you, DONE?*" he fumed, waving a futile gloved fist.

She blinked owlishly, and somehow, into her immobile cast-bronze countenance there stole a woebegone expression.

"I knew it! I just *knew* it! If anything goes wrong beautiful Bazonga . . . the only Bazonga in all the wide world, but do *they* care? Not a sniff, not a pinch, not a whisper!—" she wailed in a hollow voice.

Xarda jerked awake and stared about, blank-eyed, one small fist going for her second-best sword, salvaged from their luggage, back at the inn.

"*Wha?* Where? Have at thee, varlet' Caitiff rogue—" she broke off and stared at the magician, wide-eyed. "Where are the enemy?"

The magician cocked a thumb in the direction of the Bazonga. The Bird assumed an injured expression (somehow, don't ask me how) and uttered a loud sniff.

"*That's* the enemy," the magician snarled. "At least, she seems to be working for the wrong side! Look where she's taken us"—and he gestured below. Xarda looked over the side at league upon league of long violet grass.

"Isn't this—?"

"The Purple Plain!" the Illusionist said, scathingly. "We're way north of Yombok, even. *Scores* of leagues from where we wanted to be! It isn't possible that Ganelon could have gotten this far on his own. I am convinced the poor boy was taken captive by the Dwarves, who turned him over to the tender mercies of the Red Enchantress. She's been trying to get her hands on him since last year, when she tried to buy him from the Hegemon of Zermish."

The Bird hung her head, snuffling to herself, a woebegone expression in her eyes.

"—Blame everything on me," she whined. "Go on! — *Do.* I don't care; I just don't *care* . . ."

The Illusionist, fuming, brought his tirade to a halt. Grumbling and grexing under his breath, he glared at the shamefaced Bazona.

"Stop whimpering," he grouched. "Can't be helped now. We'll just have to turn around and go back to . . . *now* what's the matter?" he demanded suspiciously, as the Bird looked even sorrier.

"Well, you see . . . I wan't really watching while I flew . . . it *was* dark and all . . . night, you know! . . . and I'm . . . well . . . uh . . ."

"What? You're *what?*"

"I'm not at all sure which way is 'back,' " she confessed in a very small, frightened voice.

Xarda and the Illusionist stared at each other blankly. Then they turned and looked south. Endless leagues of grass, the dim glitter of the Glass Sea, and the dull, lumpy ridges of anonymous mountains was all they could see.

"Well, the Land of Red Magic could be *that* way . . ." began Xarda, tentatively.

"Sure. Or *that* way, or even *that* way," grumbled the old magician wearily. "I knew I shouldn't have gone to sleep and left this mindless, scatter-brained creature to her own devices!"

"No use crying over spilt water over the dam," said Xarda, getting her clichés somewhat mixed. "What's to be done about it, that's the question."

Prince Erigon, from the back seat, cleared his throat politely.

"I say, maybe we could ask for directions?"

"From whom?" asked the Illusionist, gloomily.

"Well, there's a city over there, east of us . . ."

"There *is?* Where?" The Illusionist craned around to look. Sure enough, some two or three miles away, built right in the very midst of the interminable grassy plains, stood the towers and ramparts of a curiously futuristic metropolis, all made of bright metal that sparkled prettily in the morning sun.

"I say, that's odd. The maps show no city anywhere around here. The Purple Plain forms a natural barrier between the many countries of Greater Zuavia and the upper borders of Northern YamaYamaLand; there's nothing on the Plains themselves, except for wandering herds of Indigons and an occasional Youk. At least, there's not supposed to be . . ."

"Maybe that was so, the last time you were in these parts, magister," said Xarda practically. "But there's certainly something there now."

"So there is," the old magician mused. "Well, I haven't been up north for ten thou-. . . for quite a few years, I mean. I suppose somebody could have built a city here, during the interim. Heaven knows a lot of people have been rendered homeless by the Ximchak Barbarians, further north . . . still, it *does* seem odd!"

"Well. Let's go over and take a look at it. From the air, I mean," said Xarda, getting bored from inaction. "We don't have to land if the people look unfriendly or dangerous. What do you say?"

The Illusionist scratched his chin with the tip of one forefinger, eddying the lavender vapors that perennially masked his features from view. "I don't know," he said thoughtfully. "Everytime we land in a strange city, seems like we get into trouble. Look at Chx. Horx, too, for that matter; of course that was before we met you, my dear, but still . . . "

"If you *hadn't* landed in Horx, and if Ganelon *hadn't* gotten into trouble trying to help me, I'd be a slave of the Holy Horxites right now," she said, with a touch of reproof. "So forgive me if I can't quite regard your experiences in Horx as an unqualified disaster—"

"Of course, my dear, I didn't mean—"

"Are we going to float here all day, while you silly humans just talk?" squawked the Bazonga bird restively. Now that they were no longer angry at her foolish flying in the wrong direction, it had not taken the ebullient vehicle long to recover her usual good spirits.

"Oh, all right, let's go," sighed the magician. "Might as well have a look at the place. Can't do any harm, I suppose."

"Tally-ho, yoicks, yoicks!" sang the Bird, happily speeding up. She curved about, Istrobian's flying kayak wobbling behind her like an aerial caboose, and flew east towards the strange metal city that Prince Erigon had noticed.

The nearer they got to it, the more curious it looked to them. The City was *all* metal—streets, towers, buildings, and everything else. And it was a lot smaller and more compact than it had looked from further off: instead of dwindling into scattered suburbs and farms at the edges, like most cities, it just stopped at a certain distance from its center. This termination was very clearly marked; in fact the city was a perfect disk, evenly trimmed around the outer perimeter. The streets that radiated out from its center like spokes from the hub of a wheel, stopped completely at the edges of the disk, ending in purple grass. There were no roads leading to it. It looked as if some playful or mischievous deity had just picked it up from somewhere and plunked it down here in the middle of nowhere, for a joke.

They flew over it, dipping and swerving to avoid the spires, while the three adventurers peered over the sides of their craft curiously. There seemed to be hardly any people out on the streets, although it was well into mid-morning by this time; you almost would have thought the city uninhabited, if that hadn't been obviously unlikely. *Somebody* had to keep the city in good repair, and all that metal polished!

Then somebody noticed them. At least, a searchlight went on in the upper tiers of the enormous centermost building. The light was a peculiar throbbing green, and it swung around to bathe them in its beam. This was pretty odd, since it was a bright, clear day.

Then the Bazonga began squawking excitedly and angrily. At the same time she began to lose altitude in a steep, headlong nose dive.

"Stop! Whoa! What are you doing, you crazy Bird?"

demanded the Illusionist, bracing himself against the forward edge of the cockpit to avoid falling out.

"Nothing: it's not *me!*" the Bird wailed. "Something's pulling me down——"

The ungainly winged vehicle hurtled groundward helplessly in the grip of some strange force. It looked as if the Bazonga would crash into the side of the central structure, but just in time an enormous trapdoor opened in the flanks of the curious structure, and the bird vehicle and her passengers were swallowed up.

The huge trapdoor closed with a metallic clang.

The odd green searchlight turned itself off.

About ten minutes later, the whole City rose up from the surface of the plain on a whooshing air-cushion and began moving away in an easterly direction, picking up speed until it was skimming along over the purple grasses at a pretty good clip.

The City moved along in one piece, because it was built as one unit. Which was very odd, because cities just aren't built that way.

But, then, it wasn't really a City at all.

# 20.

# THE ARMORY
# OF TIME

They woke deeply refreshed and somehow inwardly cleansed and renewed. It was the air of this place, thought Ganelon, lazily stretching: it was filled with magic. Dragon Magic. The oldest magic in the world, save only for that older, mightier magic whereby the very world was made.

He looked about, but neither Grrff nor the boy were visible. He must have slept longer than either of his companions, thought he. Rising, he was surprised to find a black leather war-harness, scarlet loin-cloth, girdle, boots and cloak, all laid out neatly beside the place where he had been sleeping. They were the exact duplicates of the clothes he had been wearing and had abandoned when he had fled from the Land of Red Magic. *Dragon Magic*!, he thought to himself, with a grim smile. Gratefully, he climbed into the familiar harness and buckled the straps and trappings about his mighty torso.

He came out of the cave into a green glade, dreaming in a sunlit haze and filled with birdsong. There, by the edge of a fresh, bubbling pool, the Karjixian Tigerman lay stretched out. The furry fellow had obviously just taken a dip and was sleepily drying his coat in the sun. He looked up as Ganelon came near, noticed the war-harness, and nodded towards a pile of belongings heaped beside him.

"Grrff too!" he rumbled complacently. Sitting up, he poked through the bundle until he found his weapon, which he lifted for Silvermane to see. It was a ygdraxel, the traditional weapon of the Tigermen. Ganelon grunted and nodded. Grrff lay back with a yawn.

"Grandfather Dragon is the most thoughtful of hosts," said the Tigerman. "There's breakfast over there on that rock."

Ganelon drank from the small cascade that poured down over the rocks to join the pool; the water was crisp, cold, deliciously pure. Then he ambled over to study the array of eatables. Hot-cakes and syrup steamed amidst melting *glick* butter; sausages still sizzled in a hot pan; fresh, foaming milk stood in a tall frosted tumbler.

"Where's the lad?" he asked, sitting down to eat. Grrff nodded over in one direction. "With the Old Dragon," he mumbled, "the cub's fascinated by 'im." Ganelon started to say something else, then saw that the Karjixian was settling into a doze, and returned his full attention to the superb breakfast.

A while later he found the Old One stretched out before the mouth of his cave, enjoying the dim gold sun of Faërie. He was so enormous that parts of him were lost in the forest that grew up almost to the cave's mouth. Ridges and hillocks of his vast length appeared here and there, rising out of the forest like far hills. By daylight his scales, each as huge as a knight's shield, were dark, deep green and sparkling.

Phadia sat on the broad flat nose of the Dragon, leaning back against his nostril-ridges, staring up into the great, sleepy, amused eyes of the Old One. They were chatting, and as Ganelon approached he could hear the lad's bright, clear tones over the subterranean rumble of the Dragon's voice. The giant grinned to himself. The lad was completely in awe of the ponderous old creature, yet thoroughly unafraid of him. Just to look upon a Dragon sent a creepy thrill up the boy's spine, for Dragons were to a child of his era every bit as awful, grand and mysterious as they would be to you or me.

They looked up at his approach.

*Good-morrow, Silverhair,* the Dragon greeted him affably. *Slept you well in my Deep?*

"That's the name of his cave, you know," the boy said pertly. " 'Dzimdazoul's Deep.' There used to be myths about it, the cave I mean; but that was three hundred million years ago!"

"I slept—"

"Did you bathe in the pool?" the boy chattered on. "*I* did! I was up this morning before either of you. I've been all over—except in the Armory. 'The Armory of Time', that's what *he* calls it. There are all kinds of magic weapons there, left behind by the famous heroes. Grandfather Dragon has promised to show them to me! You and Grrff can come along if you like."

Ganelon was interested, of course: fighting was, after all, his profession.

"All right," he said. "Let me go wake up Grrff."

They came into an immense gallery, cathedral-like in its reverent hush, its ghostly gleams and echoes, its shadowy and timeless serenity. Above them, a forest of slender pillars soared to join Gothic arches far overhead; the dim glory of Faërie smote through splendid windows of gules and emerald and purple glass.

The walls were of clean smooth stone, polished marble for the most part, and to these walls there were affixed many swords . . . swords almost beyond the numbering. Old they were, and well-used, their handgrips stained with the sweat and the blood of heroes, the long gleaming blades bearing many dints. Above each of these swords was set its name and history, in characters of lapis set in red-gold. And they were very famous names.

*All the swords of all the heroes that ever were or will be are hung here,* said the Old Dragon softly. *Here were they left behind by the heroes of olden myth and legend, who came trooping through the dim ways of Faërie on their way to their Reward. This wall here, below an old and shining banner called the Oriflamme, bears the charmed weapons of the heroes of France.*

*The Twelve Peers, they were called, and here at their head is bright Joyeuse, that was borne by their Emperor, Charlemagne . . . three years went into the fashioning thereof, and after him it passed to the strong hand of William of Orange. And here, beneath it, hangs proud Durandal. Vulcan, the smith of the gods, forged it for Hector the Trojan in the fires of Tartarus. When that Prince of Troy fell it was taken from his hand by Penthesilea, Queen of the Amazons, from whom it passed down the generations to her descendant, Almontes, till Roland wrested it away. His dearest friend in all the world was Oliver, and here by Durandal hangs Hautclear: once Closamont the Roman Emperor bore it on the field, but it was more bravely borne by gallant Oliver. Here hang the blades of all the other Peers: Almace that was the Bishop Turpin's sword, and Flamberge that was Renaud de Montauban's, Sauvagine the Relentless, Murgles, and bright Gloreuse that cut through the nine swords made by Ansias, and Galas, and Munifican . . . and that world-famous sword, Curtana the Short, that was made by the giant-smith, Brumadant, who forged it twenty times, and twenty times he tempered it in the blood of dragons; 'twas the great sword of Ogier the Dane, who won it from Caraheut, the King of the Saracens. And here, hung in a row beneath them, are the swords of their enemies, the Moors, Tartars and the Saracens: this is Preciuse, once owned by Baligant of Araby, and Tranchera, the magic sword of Agricane, the King of Tartary. Here is hung the thrice-enchanted Balisardo: the sorceress Falerina fashioned it wherewith to slay Roland, but she failed . . .*

They stared at the nicked and worn old blades that yet shone with the fierce, thirsty luster of sharp steel, and the names of forgotten heroes and dusty, ancient wars echoed once again in the hushed stillness. Merveilleuse the Wonderful was there, the sword of Doon de Mayence, Sanglamore and Fusberta, and the Green Sword that had been Amadis of Gaul's. They passed on to where beneath a blue, faded banner stitched with

thirteen crowns of tarnished gold, swords flashed and
gleamed and glittered.

*These are the swords of the mightiest of the heroes of
Britain*, whispered the Old Dragon. *And there, higher
than them all, hangs that most famous sword in the
world, deathless Excalibur, that was made in Avalon
for the hand of Arthur the King. See, see, its shining
splendors the long ages have not dimmed! There near it
hangs his other sword as well, Clarent, Sword of Mira-
cles . . . the Sword in the Stone! And there below are
hung in shining ranks Aroundight, the sword of Lance-
lot, and Morddure that wise Merlin made, forging its
fierce steel in the fires of Mount Aetna, tempering it
seven times in the bitter Styx . . . and many another
famous sword of England hang nearby: great Ascalon,
St. George of Merrie England's sword, and bright Mor-
glay that once Sir Bevis of Hampton bore; Corrouge,
Sir Otuel's fair blade, and many more.*

The swords of the heroes of the North they looked
upon: Sköfnung, that the sea god's daughter got from
the dwarves and gave to Hrolf Kraki, the King of the
Danes, and Goldhilt, that was young Hjalti's once; and
Egil's Drangvandil, that had been borne to wars afore-
time by Skallagrim, and Lövi, the charmed longsword
of Bjarki, and Laevatein, made with runes of power.
Tyrfing, the invincible sword of the Visigoths, that was
forged for the hero Angantyr, and Aettartangi, the
famous sword of Grettir the Strong; Gram and Nothung,
aye, and Rithil; Regin made it and it cut out Fafnir's
heart.

One wall blazed with intolerable brightness, dazzling
as the noon sun, and the swords thereon were huger
than mortal men might ever bear. Shielding his eyes
against the furious light that shone therefrom, Ganelon
asked their host of these.

*These are the swords that were borne once by the
very gods themselves . . . that mighty brand with
edges jagged as a thunderbolt is Chrysaor the Terrible,
which Zeus wielded in his war against the Titans . . .
and there is Fragarach the Answerer, the sword that*

*Lugh the Sun god bore back from the Land of the Living . . . and the swords called Great Fury and Little Fury, that were Manannan mac Lir's . . . and Balmung, which Odin gave to Sigurd the Volsung; and Odin's own grim brand, Brimir, that the giants made . . . and Frey's sword, Hundinsbana, Höfud, the god Heimdall's sword . . . and beyond them, the awful and wonderful Asidevata that was first borne by Shiva, then by Vishnu, and then by Indra . . . and Orna, sword of Tethra, that the god Ogma took in battle . . .*

They saw rare and fabulous swords: Philippan, the sword of Marc Anthony, Nagelring, the sword Dietrich of Berne got from the dwarf Alpris, Zulfiqar, the sword called Cleaver of Vertebrae which the angel Gabriel gave to Mohammed the Prophet; Dhami the Trenchant, the sword of Antar, hero of India, and Miming, made by Wayland Smith, the greatest of all makers of swords. Most were of clean bright steel, but not all: the famous Sword of Sharpness wherewith Sir Jack slew the giants Cormoran, Galligantus and Blunderbore had for its blade a razory-thin shaft of pure diamond, pale as ice; and the sword of Amadis, which they had already seen, was green as emerald; and Crocea Mors, which Julius Caesar used against Cassibelaunus when he invaded Britain, was as yellow as saffron. Strangest of all, it may be, was Hrunting, the sword of Unferth: the blade thereof was brass, dyed with drops of poison and tempered in blood; with it, in later years, Beowulf the Great slew the Ogress.

They came to one wide wall at the end of the tremendous hall. *These are the swords renowned in tale and story,* said Dzimdazoul. *Their names can mean little or naught to you . . . but here are hung forever immortal Anduril and Sacnoth, Randir and Rhindon, Glamdring and Llyr, and the Sword of Welleran . . . Graywand and Cat's Claw, Orcrist, Broadcleaver that was Osbert's sword, black, murderous Dyrnwyn, and the twin swords, Stormbringer and Mournblade . . . Frostfire, Shadowmaker, Caliburn, and Sting.*

He blinked fondly at Ganelon, who stood staring at the brilliant glitter of enchanted steel. With a nod of his massive head, the old dragon indicated one array of gleaming blades.

*Here I shall someday hang your own sword, the Silver Sword,* he said, great eyes twinkling. *Here with Azlon, Zingazar, and Sarkozan.*

As in a dream, they passed slowly out of that mighty, shadow-thronged hall, into the sun. Behind them, the famous swords, the enchanted swords, slept on through eternity to dream of old, fabulous wars, and the hands that held them once, long ago.

# 21.
# *DRAGON'S DEEP*

Time passed them by in the Halfworld with an air of dreamlike unreality; never afterwards were they able to figure out precisely how long they were the guests of Dzimdazoul.* I find it difficult to make any sense out of this, myself: Dzimdazoul had told them that here in the Halfworld, which lies outside of the world, they were beyond the reach of Time and Change. Anyway, although there were dawns and daylight, noons and nightfalls, there was no sense of time elapsing at all . . . nothing but a dreamlike, everlasting Now.

They roamed, wandered and explored. Grrff liked the forests best, remembering the jungles of his homeland. The woods were filled with curious creatures, most of whom could talk and think was well as many men, if not better. He would come back from one of these rambles full of excited stories about unicorns, centaurs, dryads and gnomes, and elves. There were many elves in the woodlands; they were, of course, the

---

* Later on, when he had a chance to compare adventures with the old magician, Ganelon became even more confused than before on this question of how much time had elapsed. It seemed to him that at least ten to twelve days had transpired between the time he flew out of Chx, and the time he left Faërie. But according to the Illusionist, only a day and a half had passed. Ganelon was never able to resolve this curious discrepancy in later years, but the Commentators on this second book of the Epic agreed by consensus that the hyperspatial tube probably collapsed time, as it did space. Maybe so, but the time equivalencies *still* do not balance out, even if Ganelon and his friends spent only a second or two in the Halfworld of Faërie. I think myself that, by going backwards in the labyrinth, instead of continuing forward, they actually came out several days before they had gone in.

virtual rulers of Faërie, although many old, retired
gods lived here as well. Dzimdazoul patiently explained that it was into the Halfworld that most of
the prehuman denizens of the Old Earth had strayed
or fled or wandered eons ago, at the end of the Silver
Age.

The seas were full of mermaids and tritons and ore-
ads; gnomes and dwarves and trolls lived under the
hills; the fairies dwelt mostly in Mommur, their ancient,
immortal capitol, but there were troops and tribes of
woods-elves that prefered the great green forests and
made their camps therein.

Ganelon spent most of his time exploring the illimitable vastness of the Old Dragon's cavern, or "deep" as
he called it. There were many marvels there, some of
which were from the Dawn of Time, and many of
which had never before been seen by men. Besides
Dzimdazoul, the caverns were the home of many other
creatures, including an old minotaur, cranky from the
gout, and an immense Piast which had come from Ire-
land before the first men came into Europe.

There was also a most amusing Cockatrice, who was
a particular friend of the Dragon's and who became
an instant favorite of Phadia's. This grouchy old creature, who was sort of like a reptilian rooster, lived
in a small side-cave where hot sulphur bubbled up
from fiery regions below: the Cockatrice, whose name
was Hshenk, had formerly lived in ancient Persia. A
relative of the famous Phoenix, he had inherited a
tendency towards immortality on his mother's side, and
had lived long enough into the Age of Man to win a
position of some importance in the mythology of Zo-
roaster, which was a matter of considerable pride to
the grouchy old monster. He liked his sulphur-pit cave
because it was always warm and dry, and he suffered
from rheumatism, it seemed.

The Cockatrice taught Phadia checkers, or an ancient form of the game which had been popular with
the antique Persians during the days of Sahm and Zal
and Rustum. Anytime Ganelon wanted to find the lad,

he would look first in Hshenk's cave; nine times out of ten the boy would be there, lying on his stomach on some old Persian carpets, playing checkers with the Cockatrice.

Finding him there one day, Ganelon stood in the entrance to the warm cave, smiling a little at the scene. Phadia was wriggling on his tummy, kicking his heels in the air and giggling with both hands over his mouth, for he had just won another game from the old Cockatrice and the cranky old fellow was cussing a blue streak. Of course, his notion of swearing was to name half the devils in the Zoroastrian mythology, which meant nothing to Phadia, but it *was* funny to watch. When Hshenk got mad enough to cuss, his barbed tail curled up tight and his bright red coxcomb, which usually hung down floppily over one eye giving him a rakish air, stood stiffly erect and vibrated.

Between bursts of delighted giggling from Phadia, Silvermane could hear the creaky, shrill voice of the old Cockatrice, complaining furiously.

"Ahriman cook yer gizzard, lad, ye've done it again! Aeshma Daeva broil yer ear-lobes, you've done whupped me for the third time terday! Mitox an' Vereno snatch ye bald, if I'll letcher win a fourth time . . . nosiree! Set 'em up, set 'em up, ye little rascal; I'll whup ye this time, Akatasha fry me if'n I don't!"

"Oh, Uncle Hshenk! You don't really want to play another game," protested the lad between giggles.

"Paromaiti burn me if'n I don't! Set 'em up, ye scalawag, and I'll teach ye to play *real* checkers! If'n it warn't fer this cussed rheumatiz I'd of won 'em all, by Zaurvan's iron liver!"

Watching from the entrance to the cave, Ganelon studied the child with a fond eye. Even a few days away from the perfumed hothouse atmosphere of the Red Queen's palace had brought a welcome change in little Phadia. For the last two days the boy had forgotten to put on any make-up (well, perhaps just a touch of eye-liner, but that was all), and right now he looked adorably boyish—like a *real* boy, that is. His blond curls were tousled and uncombed, he had a nice scratch on his knee, and his cheek was dirty with a smudge which he had carelessly wiped with the back of his hand. Ganelon regarded the boy with avuncular satisfaction: a little more of this sort of life and the stifling, constricting influence of his former life would really begin to fade, as the lad grew and changed in wholesome, boyish directions.

He hated to interrupt the happy scene, but it was time to go. He had determined that this very morning; wakening from a deep, restful sleep he had lain there looking up at the ceiling, wondering how the Illusionist Nerelon, the girl knight of Jemmerdy and Prince Erigon fared. And somehow he had known, right then and there, that this brief, pleasant respite from their adventurings was over. He said as much, as soon as Phadia and the Cockatrice looked up from their game and noticed him.

Phadia sighed, a little depressed, but made no complaints. He worshipped the great bronze giant and was used to doing what other people wanted him to do, without whining or complaining about it. Surprisingly, it was Hshenk who raised the loudest fuss about their leaving. The grouchy old fellow had become terribly attached to the little boy, but even he saw they couldn't stay forever in Faërie: mortals could be happy here only for a time, and only to a certain extent.

"By Spenta Mainyu's goldy crown, but I'll be sad to see ye go! This here place ain't been half so lively in a million years, 'afore ye folks come! *One* good thing about it: I'll hafta go back to playin' checkers wif th' Old Dragon; and *he* let's an ol' feller win a game er two, oncet in a while! *(Sniff!)* 'Taint nothin', boy—a cinder in me eye, likely. *(Snuff!)* Git along wif ye now! An' may Holy Ormazd watch over ye lad, and yew too, big feller. Say goodbye to thet thar cat-feller fer me. *(Snmff!)* Carmaiti an' Khashathra bless 'e all."

They had a little difficulty finding Grrff, who was up in the hills. And considerably more difficulty in persuading him to come down. It seems he had struck up a relationship with a friendly lady Sphinx who lived on a cliff-top nearby; half-human female and half-lioness, she was the nearest thing to a Tiger-woman the lonely Karjixian had met in quite a while. The love-smitten Xombolian was on the verge of proposing when Ganelon came climbing up to persuade him to come down. Their yowls of farewell set the canyons to ringing and Grrff came down slowly, grumpily, with many a languishing backwards look, refused to be consoled, and sulked for the next hour and a half.

The Old Dragon was coiled sleepily atop his mound of treasure, just where he had been when they had first encountered him.

*I knew you would be going home soon, anxious to rejoin your friends,* he said in his hissy, thunder-rumbly voice. *I shall miss thee, manlings; aye, and mightily! So few come into Faërie in these sad, latter days . . .*

There were presents for them all, of course: the new clothing and gear they had found beside them that first morning when they awoke, a broadsword for Ganelon, (but not an enchanted one), and a fine knife for Phadia, in a case of genuine dragonskin.* And the Old Dragon had packed a nice lunch. They made their farewells awkwardly and the boy cried.

*Get along with you, now! Your friends are becoming worried as to what has happened, and you have much unfinished business to tend to. Through the archway, as before—but backwards this time, mind you! Two short steps back, then one big step to your left. Farewell, now, for a while. Mayhap we shall all meet again, another day!*

His great, pebbly eyelids drooped sleepily, eclipsing the green moon-eyes as, hand in hand, they backed

---

* Dragons shed their scaly hide twice a millennium, you know, as snakes do a couple times a year. So the scabbard for Phadia's knife was *probably* made from one of Dzimdazoul's own castings. (This is a speculation you will find in the Thirtieth Commentary; Bariche agrees it is more than likely correct, and even Nruntha was unable to refute it satisfactorily.)

cautiously into the stone arch whose keystone was marked with the Omega Triskelion.

The dimly-lit half-circle that was the Dragon's Deep when seen from the other side of the portal receded from them weirdly, dwindling to a remote point of greenish luminescence before it winked out, leaving them standing in pitch-black darkness. But the last glimpse they caught of him, the Old One was settling down for another million-year nap.

They left him sleeping. And stepped backward, to the left, and into the world again.

# Book Four

~~~~~~~~~~~~~~~~~~~~~~~~~~~~~

# THE MOBILE CITY
# OF KAN ZAR KAN

*The Scene:* **The Purple Plain on the Border between Northern Yama-YamaLand and Greater Zuavia; the Machine City.**

*New Characters:* **Slioma, Yemple, Zilth, and other Iomagoths; the City Itself; Fryx again.**

# 22.

# SHANGHAIED, OR SOMETHING

Black, whirling darkness closed down upon the three adventurers and enveloped them. The greenlit archway, with its vista of the Dragon curled in his Deep, receded to a dim spark and vanished.

They stepped backwards in unison. The abysmal blackness was more like a total cessation of the powers of sight, rather than any absence of light itself. And with it came a giddy sensation, a feeling of vertigo, which they could not recall having experienced before. Perhaps it was due to the fact that they were retracing their steps, rather than going forward; at any rate, they took the sideways step as Dzimdazoul had counseled and, very suddenly, with no sense of transition or no idea of quite how they had gotten there, found themselves standing on a level plain, knee-deep in meadow grass.

Ganelon hefted his weapon and glanced about, blinking at the swiftness of this peculiar mode of transportation. In every direction a featureless plain of purple grass stretched, from horizon to horizon.

He turned to look behind him. A black vortex hung unsupported in the air, slowly fading. The bottom-most whorl of the whirlpool of inkiness was level with the plain itself. Above the upper curve of the vortex of darkness, the Omega Triskelion hung as if suspended in mid-air by an enchanter's art.

The vortex faded and was gone. Now there was

nothing behind them but empty leagues of long grass blowing in the wind.

The hour was early morning, he assumed, from the dewy freshness of the air and the cold, wet touch of the nodding plumes of grass that brushed against his bare knees. The sun was a dim, faint red-gold disk at the very edge of the world, in the direction he presumed to be the east.

Ganelon had not the faintest notion of where the hyperspatial tube had deposited them, and he said as much to Grrff when the Tigerman, looking puzzled, inquired.

"Well, wherever we are, it doesn't look like Dwarfland, or the domain of the Red Bitch," growled the Karjixian. "But where *are* we—and why did we come out here?"

"Nor does it look like Ning, or Holy Horx, or the country of the Chxians," mused Silvermane. "And it certainly isn't any part of the Hegemony, or the Voormish Desert, or even Karjixia! In fact, the only country I've ever heard of that's supposed to look anything like this is the Purple Plain itself—"

"The Purple Plain?" grumbled the Tigerman, wrinkling his snout distastefully. "Isn't that where the Indigons are supposed to herd? Why would the Labyrinth let us out *here?* Why, it's way up north, isn't it? Grrff's heard tell of it before."

Ganelon nodded, his face expressionless, black eyes moody.

"What did the Old Dragon say? Something about 'your friends will be getting anxious about you,' or words to that effect. I don't know about your friends, but mine ought to be back in Chx, or flying around Dwarfland and the Land of Red Magic, hunting for me; at least, I presume the Dragon was talking about my master, Xarda and that prince fellow. But if this *is* the Purple Plain, it's way up north as you said, beyond Yombok and all those countries. I can't imagine why master would come here . . . we were on our way to the kingdom of Jemmerdy, really."

"And Jemmerdy is down south, next to Parvania," muttered the Tigerman. "Well . . . here we are, and here we're going to stay, Grrff guesses! The question is—not why we got transported here—but what we're supposed to do now that we *are* here?"

They looked around, without any ideas in particular. For as far as the eye could see in any direction, there was nothing else to be seen, except league on league of blowing grass rippling under the invisible caress of the wind. The sky which arched above them was as empty as the plain whereon they stood. Gold and crimson appeared in the direction they assumed to be the east; the sky was still dark purple directly overhead, but gradually the flush of rosy dawn illuminated the dome of heaven.

"All I can suggest is to go south," Ganelon confessed after some moments of silent cogitation. "South of here, somewhere, is Jemmerdy. And if my master has given up trying to find me, that's where he would go. We were taking Xarda home. Xarda is one of those lady knights they have in Jemmerdy . . . you know, that's the country where the men are all artists, and intellectuals, and the women do the hard work and the fighting."

Griff nodded; he had heard of Jemmerdy.

"So . . . if that's east, which it must be, then back there must be south. And we might as well get started, as we have a lot of walking to do. It'll be easier in early morning, before the heat of the day comes upon us . . ."

Phadia had contributed exactly nothing to this desultory conversation. The boy was too busy looking around at this newness, and anyway, he was accustomed to leaving all of the decisions in his life to grown-ups. Since leaving the hothouse atmosphere of the Pueratorium, in which everything always remained exactly the same and nothing was ever different or particularly exciting, the lad had gone through a remarkable series of strange, marvelously new experiences. He regarded the whole thing as a lark, a spree:

it was, in fact, the first real holiday he had ever known, and he was enjoying it enormously.

Just standing here like this, up to your tummy in damp grass, was new and strange and therefore, exciting to him. Whatever was going to happen next was a matter of complete indifference to him. If his new friends wanted to march south all day, well, he would march along with them as best he could.

Blue clear sky . . . red-and-gold sunrise . . . empty expanses of cool, dewy grass . . . he was eagerly determined to enjoy everything. The decisions were made by the grown-ups; which was, he thought to himself in a satisfied way, the way things ought to be.

So they started walking south.

The city caught up to them before they had been walking for a half-hour. Phadia had been the first to glimpse it, moving swiftly and almost silently across the plains. His companions had regarded it with great amazement, for even on Old Earth's last and mightiest continent, in these days of the Twilight of Time, a City that moved along overland all by itself was an object of considerable rarity.

At first, they simply continued along the way they had been heading before the weird, hovering metal metropolis appeared on the horizon. And at first the City moved in a straight line, evidently following a course which ran divergent to their own.

But before very long the City turned about and came towards them, and they realized they had been seen or sensed by whatever creatures might be the inhabitants of the futuristic mobile metropolis. They began to run, but in a little while they abandoned this attempt as futile. It became obvious that the Mobile City could traverse the Purple Plains many times faster than could they.

There was nowhere to hide, nowhere to take a stand, not even a tree to climb. So they just stood there waiting for the City to approach them. Ganelon and the Tigerman stood side by side, their weapons held at the ready; as for the boy, he cowered timidly behind the bronze giant, peeping out from time to time.

The City came cruising up on its whooshing air-cushion until its perimeter was about thirty feet away from them. Then it came to a dead halt. They stood staring up at it, the slim, soaring spires and towers like truncated cones, and peculiarly-shaped domes which were rather like Christmas tree ornaments. A network of aerial bridges or walkways curved between the domes, spires and towers. But there seemed to be no traffic upon these, neither were there to be seen any guards or sentries stationed on the rooftops of the nearer structures. In fact, they could see no people at all. Not one figure was visible on the long straight streets which radiated from the central ziggurat-like edifice in all directions, like the spokes of a wheel. It was all very mysterious, and quite alarming.

A few moments later, elongated metal shafts extruded from beneath the nearest edge of the immense metal plate which formed the foundation of the City as a whole. These tubes telescoped smoothly towards them with a faint, creaking sound: the whiff of lubricating oil reached their nostrils.

The tubes extended themselves until they were directly above the three: then wriggling pseudopods of gleaming red metal came slithering out of the open tip of the rods. These extrusions were supple and boneless as are the tentacles of a Myriapod *, and they came wriggling down around the three motionless figures. Ganelon saw that they were about as thick as his thumb and seemed to be made of overlapping sequences of metal rings, which slid smoothly upon each other. They were perhaps held together by some cohesive force, such as magnetism.

---

\* An example of lapse of internal time-sense, on the part of the author or authr (or authors) of the Epic. That is, Ganelon had yet to encounter a Myriapod at this point in the course of his career. He does not fight a Myriapod, in fact, until the eighth book of the Gondwane Epic.

As the metal tendrils settled about them, Ganelon voiced his booming war cry and struck at them with his sword. The sword, which was made of ferrous metal, struck the tendrils and clung thereto, as if in the grip of some unbreakable force. Simultaneously, the Tigerman had employed his ygdraxel in a comparable maneuver, with precisely the same result. Or lack of result, I should say.

The metal tentacles slithered about them, coiling about hips, upper chest, arms and legs. They were gripped snugly, but not with crushing force. Held immobile and helpless, but not uncomfortably so, the three struggling figures were lifted smoothly up into the air, whereupon the telescoping rods began to close up with a jerky, machine-like motion.

They were borne in this manner up onto the edge of the Mobile City, which still hovered about fifteen feet above the surface of the plain on its air-cushion. When the tendril-system had reached the edge of the city, it passed them on into the grip of a metal net which two mechanical arms, branching out from the upper story of a cylindrical building of some kind, held open to receive them. They were suspended for a moment over the open net, then the tendrils released their multiple grips. They tumbled into the flexible container, whose mesh gave with a springy elasticity under their weight. The mechanical arms thereupon drew closed the mouth of the net, which it then passed on to the next waiting pair of arms. In this manner they were passed from "hand" to "hand" across the width of the City, until they reached the central ziggurat. An opening appeared in its curved flanks and they were dumped within.

As they tumbled into the circular opening, Ganelon was trying to figure out whether a mechanical flying city had kidnapped them, or captured them, or was it that they had been shanghaied?

The precise term, of course, was irrelevant.

They were prisoners.

# 23.
# THE WELCOMING COMMITTEE

Dumped into the circular orifice which opened in the gleaming metal flanks of the central ziggurat, Ganelon and his two comrades went tumbling head-first down a slick, smooth slide. This incline carried them down into the bowels of the structure in a giddy, swooping ride that curved and twisted in the most bewildering manner. For the most part, the slide led them through regions of lightless gloom; but at intervals they shot forth into the blue-white glare of artificial lamps. During such periods they went dizzyingly past, or through, or around levels filled with incomprehensible machinery. There were giant engines, motors whose bulk dwarfed the largest mammals, and confluences of colossal pipes and tubes which resembled nothing so much as titanic pumping stations.

After some time their trip ended most abruptly as the slide terminated in mid-air, hurtling them onto an immense inflated cushion or gas-bag obviously designed to minimize injury.

No sooner had they struggled to their feet than lassos fell around them, tightening with a jerk. Staring up, they were surprised to see a number of disreputable-looking, rather ruffianly figures suspended above them, clinging to an aerial network of bright-blue metal pipes and tubes. They were a rag-tag, roguish lot, clad in the filthy tatters of former finery, wild greasy locks flying around pinched faces. Quite obviously, these dilapidated vagabonds were stationed

151

here to seize or subdue any chance visitors to the moving metropolis who might happen to drop in, as you might say. It was equally obvious that the scrawny rogues counted heavily on their prey being stunned and dazed by their swooping, veering journey down the steep inclines.

In the present case they had erred, at least as far as the burly Tigerman went. Like all of his feline ancestors, Grrff had the ability to land on his feet and his sense of balance was innate, as was his natural-born resistance to vertigo. Voicing a rumbling roar of outrage, the brawny Karjixian writhed out of his bonds in a trice. He had lost his ygdraxel to the magnetic tendrils, but being unarmed never phased the jungle warrior. Reaching up, he seized ahold of the lasso cords and gave them a vigorous pull, snatching two squeaking ragamuffins from their precarious perch in the piping. They fell squalling and bouncing onto the gas-cushion and Grrff sprang upon them, buffetting them senseless with his heavy paws.

Ganelon was dizzy and disoriented from his headlong trip down the greased shoot, but he was only a moment or two behind the Tigerman's example. One powerful jerk of his arms and four of the raggedy starvelings were plucked from their places above. The others, shrilling curses, clambered away from the debacle with the ungainly agility of monstrous spiders, abandoning their hapless cronies to whatever fate lay in store for them.

Ganelon quickly subdued his four captives in much the same manner as had Grrff and, turning to see how Phadia fared, was pleased to discover that the resourceful lad had whipped out his knife and had cut himself free. Of them all, only Phadia had not been disarmed by the magnetic tendrils which had captured them.

Gripping his captives by the scruff of the neck, Ganelon floundered to the edge of the immense inflated cushion and slid down it to the floor of the huge, basement-like room in which the greased slides had deposited them. Grrff came at his heels, kicking his unconscious catch along ahead of him, and Phadia brought up the rear.

"A fine welcoming committee!" fumed Grrff, his usually amiable temper severely ruffled for once. "If these skinny varlets be an example of the local citizenry, then we have fallen into a lair of bandits!" He gave his unconscious captives a furious shake, then began searching them curiously.

"Not bandits," Ganelon corrected him, lips pursed judiciously. "Iomagoths, I should say. Notice the tribal tattoo above the left eye. But this is strange! The Iomagoths are generally a kindly and hospitable lot, so long as you keep your eye on them and lock up the family silver."

"What are Iomagoths?" inquired the boy, bright-eyed with curiosity. He found their endless succession of adventures a source of continuous entertainment.

"Wandering bands of tinkers who travel the countryside in gaudy carts, drawn by *nguamodons*," replied the Construct. "Ages ago, they were a horde of barbarians who formerly inhabited the regions known as The Hegemony. As the other denizens of those lands gradually became civilized, the Iomagothic clans retained their nomadic way of life. But they were weaned over many generations from their war-like ways, becoming a gaudy, thievish, lazy, illiterate race of wanderers. I have never known them to dwell in cities before; wonder how they came to be here?"

"Probably snatched up in passing by this mechanical kleptomaniac we are all traveling in," growled Grrff disdainfully. "Harmless tinkers, is it? Maybe in your homeland, big man; in Grrff's dear country, they are chicken-thieves, cattle-rustlers, and *kaobonga*-stealers!" *

A few of the captives were beginning to come

---

* A species of very large, four-legged, air-breathing fish found in the jungle streams and rivers of Karjixia, and cultivated by the Tigermen as a staple food.

around. Groaning piteously and clutching throbbing brows, they crouched on bony, trembling haunches and stared fearfully at the somber, towering young giant and the burly-chested Tigerman.

Licking thin lips with the point of his tongue, one of them hesitantly addressed them.

"S-surely, your wor-worships intend no h-harm to a poor old Iomagoth?" this individual piped shrilly, sharp little black eyes darting about as if seeking an avenue of escape. "No h-harm was meant to your noble persons, Zilth assures you! 'Tis our practice to immobilize unexpected visitors, in order to ascertain if they be enemies or f-friends—"

" 'Immobilize,' is it, you scrawny guttersnipe?" growled the Tigerman threateningly. "Grrff'll 'immobilize' you, aye, with his claws out, next time you try to jump us!" And, thrusting his great paws under the little man's nose, he bared his glittering and savagely sharp claws with a *snicc* sound, making the little rogue squeak and cower.

"No rough stuff, Grrff," cautioned Ganelon, stepping forward. "We can't get any information out of these creatures if you scare them half out of their wits! You, there, Zilth, is it? Who's in charge of this city?"

The little man huddled at his feet, examining his second interlocutor with bright, fearful eyes.

"The noble gentleman asks a question with two answers, at least," he whimpered. "The City runs itself, of course; it's name is Kan Zar Kan. But we of The Folk who dwell herein like hunted rabbits, well, our chief rules us. King Yemple is his name . . . "

"No one lives here but you Iomagoths, then?"

The little rogue darted his eyes about and licked his lips as he did, seemingly by reflex action, before every spurt of speech. Ganelon got the feeling that, for Zilth, every direct question gave him the choice between his normal mode of reply, a devious lie, and that rarity from his lips—truth. Under the present circumstances, it seemed, he was too frightened to speak anything but the truth.

"Mostly Iomagoths," he said in a reluctant whine. "A few rogues, of course—"

"Who eluded your clutches in much the same manner as we did?" offered Silvermane. The scrawny little man eyed him warily, then nodded.

His bony wrists tied behind his back, Zilth reluctantly led them towards the headquarters of the Iomagoths. The others they had seized were disarmed of a staggering cumulative arsenal of daggers, dirks, stilettos, and a number of wicked little hook-knives. They were bound, gagged and left behind.

The room into which they had been precipitated was an enormous, meandering sort of sub-basement, dark and poorly ventilated, and thronged with an immensity of hydraulic pipes, tubes and conduits. The floor was of oil-stained concrete. Why the City had deposited them in such a place was unknown to the Iomagoths, who had only been in residence for about two generations, having been captured by the Mobile City pretty much as Grrff had guessed. They had been crossing the Purple Plain in one of their gypsy caravans forty years ago when suddenly, the City had descended upon them and snatched them up into its metal maw, one by one. And here they had remained ever since, either too fearful to attempt to leave, or frustrated in doing so. The City tolerated their presence not so much because it liked them, but because it felt that a proper city should have inhabitants, and any inhabitants were better than no inhabitants.

All this was elicited from their little captive during the subterranean journey. Once his fears of lingering torture or sudden death were mollified, the scrawny little rogue became actually talkative. He was a remarkable little person, no more than four feet tall and thin as a broomstick, with a long-jawed, unshaven face and a sallow, unhealthy complexion. Since his beard was blue-black, this lent him the most peculiar appearance you can imagine. The upper part of his face was yellow, and the bottom half a stubbly blue.

He had a long sharp nose, bright inquisitive black eyes, and lank blue-black, remarkably greasy hair, bound about his brows by a scarlet kerchief. Gold rings wobbled in his earlobes and his breath exuded a mingled redolency of garlic, onions, cheese and sour wine.

He did not, of course, say so, but Ganelon guessed that when it had been observed by lookouts that the Mobile City was in the process of scooping up another shanghaied "citizen," a troop of the gypsies went down to the gas-cushion room. They readied themselves to capture the new recruit, strip him of his possessions and then, as likely as not, conduct him before the princeling of the vagabonds as a potential slave. Possibly some of the Kan Zar Kanians enlisted into the local citizenry in this fashion were later ransomed, or perhaps joined the tinker band voluntarily. That remained to be seen.

In the meanwhile, Ganelon just clumped along gloomily, following where the capering, voluble little rogue led. He wondered what had become of the Illusionist, Xarda and Erigon. Were they captives here, or had the City slain them?

Or were they in Kan Zar Kan at all?

That remained to be seen.

# 24.

# WITHIN THE ROBOT CITY

Yemple was a fat, jolly old man with a pink-yellow scalp visible through his sparse strands of dirty white hair. His rubicund face was perpetually wreathed with sunny smiles, but despite his air of heartiness Ganelon sensed a clever, cunning brain that ticked away under the surface, constantly estimating the advantages and drawbacks in whatever situation presented itself.

Probably Ganelon was correct in guessing that it was the usual thing for the Iomagoths to seize upon, plunder and enslave newcomers to Kan Zar Kan the moment the automatic mechanism deposited them in the basement of the central edifice. If so, the gypsy king accepted the complete reversal of roles with equanimity, beyond a few bawdy jests at the expense of poor Zilth who grinned and snickered shamefacedly, shuffling his long feet in embarrassment.

They were served a buffet lunch which consisted of prairie-birds roasted whole, feathers and all; air vegetables, a variety of succulent tuber which floated at various levels above the Plains suspended from inflated bladders filled with a hydrogenous gas; and shishke-babs, consisting of gamy meat cubes skewered and cooked over charcoal. Half-heartedly chewing on this last delicacy, Ganelon wisely decided not to inquire into its source. Since the Iomagoths inhabited the sewers of the robot metropolis doubtless those sewers, like all others within Ganelon's experience, were inhabited by rats.

The meal was washed down with a thin, sour red wine, to the tinkling thumps of tambourines and the hip-wrigglings of dancing-girls. Among these, the stellar role was filled by Yemple's own daughter, the lissome Slioma. She was a slim but well-rounded lass with dusky skin, flashing black eyes, and warm red lips perpetually open in a lazy, inviting smile, baring teeth of startling perfection and whiteness. Phadia, a severe critic when it came to the fine art of terpsichorean endeavor, was captivated by the vivacious princess of the gypsies, who was not very much older than himself. The lad had hardly ever seen a girl before, much less one of his own age, and his fascination proved there was hope for him yet.

As the boy watched her undulate about the room, bare brown legs twinkling amidst the twirling of flounced, scarlet, innumerable petticoats, Ganelon and Grrff observed his entranced, open-mouthed admiration. They beamed fondly and exchanged a grin of paternal satisfaction.

As the wine bottles went back and forth, the hospitable gypsy king waxed talkative. The Mobile City, he understood, was one of the remarkable constructions abandoned by the Technarchs of Vandalex after the collapse of their empire. Originally, the gigantic robot had been designed as a self-mobile, completely automatic metals mine. Equipped with electronic sensors of extraordinary subtlety, the robot mining machine was supposed to navigate the Purple Plain seeking out subterranean ore deposits. Upon finding one, it squatted atop the ground, rather like a nesting hen, extruding from its underneath drill-probes and clutchers. Excavating the ore, which it drew up into its innards, the giant robot smelted and refined the metals thus extracted from the bowels of the planet, stacking them in neatly aligned ingots.

Once programmed for these multiple functions, the machine could virtually run itself forever. When a portion of its machinery broke down through neglect or decay, the machine was permitted by its standard code of operating procedures to draw upon its stockpile of ingots, set into operation its machine-shops and thus to repair itself. In the long ages since the collapse of Vandalex and the fall of the Technarchs, the giant robot had received no further instructions from Grand Phesion, the capitol. It had been left to its own devices. Becoming over-burdened by the ingot stockpiles, the mining robot had added to its own structure, in lieu of instructions to the contrary. Observing from afar the cities of men, and lacking any other idea, the simple machine had transformed itself into the replica of a city. Since cities require inhabitants, the machine had captured a quantity of them. Its first inhabitants had been a lengthy caravan-train from Jashp, bearing a party of Zealots on pilgrimage to the shrine of the Floating Stones in far-off Klish.

The Zealots had inhabited the city for about one generation, but had died out due to a lack of females. Thereafter, the Mobile City of Kan Zar Kan (so christened by the unhappy Zealots, who named it after the most excruciating of the seventy-three hells in their dire mythology) had been careful to take aboard females as well as males, during her/his/its periodic efforts to add new citizens to the collection. The Iomagoths had replaced a dwindling band of Quaylies, one or two of which were still around.

Ganelon found it impossible to get a word in, so talkative was the fat old vagabond prince when in his cups. By the time a tattered band of giggling, bright-eyed gypsy children led them off to the sleeping quarters reserved for guests, he still had not been able to find out if any of his missing friends were also aboard the Mobile City.

He reasoned that they must be, for surely Dzimdazoul had directed them into that part of the Purple Plain for the avowed purpose of reuniting him with his friends. He went to sleep still worrying about it.

The next day, Ganelon and his companions explored the City. The gypsies were engaged in hunting meat, and the travellers rather squeamishly preferred *not* to know how their ruffianly hosts procured food for the table. Declining the invitation to join in the hunt, they were left to their own devices.

Slioma volunteered to be their guide on the tour. The bright-eyed gypsy girl was intrigued by the strangers, who represented ways of life entirely foreign to her experience. Like many girls her age, the thought of far-off lands and strange kingdoms was irresistibly exotic to her, and she had taken to tagging about after them. She proved a lively, amusing guide, with her piquant chatter and provocative, sideward glances.

She led them to the street-level of the City, which was completely deserted, save for machines. Here were built rows on rows of metal houses, or what closely resembled houses. It puzzled Silvermane that the Iomagoths ignored these relatively palatial dwellings for the dark, noisome sewers below the streets. Inquiring of Slioma on this point, the girl seemed baffled; Ganelon at length came to the conclusion that the vagabonds were more accustomed to a furtive life in hiding, than an open, lawful existence in respectable surroundings. It seemed never to have occurred to them to switch their homes to live in the upper air.

Peering inside one of the metal houses, he realized there was more good sense to their preference for the submunicipal warrens than he had at first supposed. For the houses, though neat, light, airy and scrupulously clean, were totally devoid of any furnishings, nor were there interior rooms. They were merely empty containers, whose facades alone suggested their purpose was to accomodate human families.

"Why, it must be the City's fault!" exclaimed Phadia eagerly. "Of course! The City could only see houses in other cities from a distance, and had no idea what was supposed to be inside of them!"

" 'S' true," the girl chimed in. "Ol' City 'nt know how real folks live. 'N' always cleanin' up after folks, so." She shuddered fastidiously. Personal cleanliness was a trait observed principally by strict avoidance, among her raffish tribe.

As they explored the perfectly empty buildings, strolled along the spotless but untraveled streets and ventured on some of the nearest aerial walkways, the City observed them benignly from its thousands of "eyes"—binocular vision lenses stationed at odd points about the metal metropolis. These twinkled down at them with a sentient watchfulness that made Grrff's nape-fur tingle and his hackles rise. But the continuous observation was somehow kindly and gratified. The City desired to be inhabited, and it pleased the gigantic robot intelligence to see its populace strolling about its usually unpopulated ways.

When they wearied after a time and sought to rest, a bubble car came smoothly to a halt before them and opened its transparent canopy invitingly. Phadia would have clambered in for the pleasures of an aerial ride but Grrff held him back by the scruff of the neck and Slioma indignantly waved the vehicle on its way.

"Go 'long with you," the girl scolded shrilly. "*Git,* now!" The vehicle regarded them calmly but with a trace of sadness in its lenses, then scooted off and floated into the air to join its empty, purposelessly circling comrades. The girl flirted her skirts after it, then came swaggering back to where they stood.

"Ol' cars, they take un where *they* want un to go! Nemine where *you* wanna go!" Ganelon studied the circling swarm of weightless vehicles and observed the traffic pattern, which was utterly regular He repressed a sudden qualm: had they accepted a ride from the car, they might have remained trapped in it for days or even weeks, helplessly held captive aloft until the balance of the pattern decreed their vehicle should come to rest.

During their tour of the Mobile City, Ganelon and Grrff observed with avuncular fondness the frequent and meaningful glances the girl exchanged with the boy. During one pause for rest, Phadia showed Slioma some of his cosmetics. The girl delightedly submitted to the deft application of eye-liner, lip-rouge, and instant hair-setting spray which turned her lank, greasy locks into a glossy cloud of shimmering ebon curls. Sniffing with delight the perfume he had dabbed on her wrists, the girl swore with pleasure.

A while later, looking back to see why they were lingering behind, Ganelon was amused to see them holding hands as they strolled dreamily along after the grown-ups.

The central citadel of the City interested him. Inquiring thereof, he noticed the gypsy girl evaded direct answers with slurred half-statements. As the shades of afternoon began lengthening towards nightfall, and they started to return to the submunicipal warrens for the evening meal, Ganelon directed his companions to return without him. Once they had vanished into the sewers, he headed directly towards the immense structure which bulked at the hub of the city's disk. It was there, he reasoned, that the sensory and cognitional faculties of Kan Zar Kan must be located. As the City seemed benevolent towards its denizens, he hoped to persuade the monster mechanism to assist him in locating the Illusionist.

There did not seem to be any entrance at street-level, so he clambered up the gleaming flanks to the second story and gained entry through a port which opened into a completely darkened chamber.

He had only advanced five steps into the darkness when a stern voice bade him halt. He whirled about lithely, prepared to give battle to whatever sentry was stationed here.

Light appeared amidst the darkness and by its glare Ganelon could see the being who had accosted him. He gaped in amazement at what he saw.

# 25.

# KAN ZAR KAN
# IS ATTACKED

Griff only nibbled at his dinner and drank only a flagon or two of the sour yellow wine the Iomagoths distilled from the juices of the air vegetables. The burly Tigerman was distracted by worry over the fact that Ganelon Silvermane had yet to return to the gypsy camp.

As to exactly why this should worry him, Grrff himself could not articulate. Surely, the bronze giant was able to take care of himself should he be set upon by beasts or human foes, for he was twice the weight of an ordinary man and had almost the strength of a god. The City itself, though capricious and at times inscrutable, was charitably disposed towards its inhabitants to the extent of extracting water from the atmosphere to serve their needs here in the sewers. The gypsy king assured him that Kan Zar Kan would not attempt to harm the giant man.

Still, Grrff could not allay his suspicions that something had happened to the big man he regarded as his friend, comrade and fellow-warrior. At the evening feast, peering around at the scrawny ruffians, Grrff found himself wondering if the vagabonds were really as friendly as they seemed. Perhaps they had waylaid Silvermane once he was alone, and had imprisoned or slain him. King Yemple swilled down wine, gurgling with laughter over the grotesque capers of his clowns and conjurers; sly, thievish Zilth gorged on fresh meat, jested and snickered with his cronies; Phadia and Sli-

163

oma hardly touched their meat and had eyes only for each other. Before the feast was actually concluded, the Tigerman noticed, the lad and the girl stole off together to find an unused cubicle. Grrff only hoped it was for the purpose of mutual amatory pleasure, and not a cunning plot on the part of Yemple's bravos to separate them one by one and then capture them. But about an hour and half later his tentative suspicions were relieved when the two young people returned to the feast, flushed, bright-eyed and tousled, with their clothing considerably in disarray.

By bedtime the giant man still had not returned to the tunnel system. Grrff, tossing and turning restlessly on his pallet, entertained visions of Ganelon trapped in a bubble car and condemned to endless circlings of the City; of Ganelon lost in the sewers, having forgotten the code markings which clearly blazoned the way into portions of the system currently inhabited by the Iomagoths; of Ganelon seized by the cold, dispassionate sentience of the City Brain, and now stretched naked under blazing antiseptic lamps while the robot intelligence scrutinized his innards, laid bare by dissection. The multiplicity of dire eventualities his fevered imagination conjured up forbade Grrff from slumbering.

At length he rose, took up his gear, and found his way past snoring vagabonds to the upper levels again. He had no real idea of where Ganelon Silvermane could have gotten to, nor even why the big man had remained behind. But remembering his queries regarding the central edifice, Grrff decided to begin his search there.

The City by night was weird and more than a little spooky, the faithful Tigerman discovered. The empty buildings stared at him with blank windows, like the eye-sockets of so many giant skulls. His footsteps clanged hollowly on the metal streets as he strode their length. He constantly had a feeling of being watched from a secret place of concealment by hidden eyes, which caused his hackles to lift in a stiff ruff of fur. Clenching his weapon in his huge paws he prowled the City, eyes roaming nervously from side to side.

The City was in motion, skimming along over the Purple Plain in a north-easterly direction insofar as he could judge, and traveling along at a pretty fair clip—about thirty miles per hour, he estimated roughly. The omnipresent hum and purr of the internal mechanisms of Kan Zar Kan were lost in the rush of wind that blew, with an eerie moaning sound, through the tall spires of the robot metropolis. The air-cushion which lifted the dish-like foundation of the City a dozen feet above the violet sward was almost completely soundless: the City glided across the prairie in ghostly flight. It was all just a bit unnerving, he found.

And so was the metal metropolis itself. For its un-lighted and long rows of dark, empty houses, unil-luminated towers and gloom-filled domes lent it something of the aspect of a dead, long-deserted city of the past. In his quests and peregrinations across the mighty face of Gondwane, the Tigerman had once visited the Cylinder Cities of the north and the Dead Cities of Caostro in the remote southlands: the same weird uncanniness gripped him now that he had ex-perienced in those far kingdoms, whose builders had belonged to races long since extinct.

Grrff wondered to himself why Kan Zar Kan did not light itself by night. Surely the several techniques of artificial illumination were not beyond the skills of its automatic workshops. He brooded over the pos-sibilities of their being some arcane and mysterious reason for the lack of night lights. The City, cloaked in gloom, glided across the meadowlands in an almost furtive fashion. As if bound on a sinister mission, it concealed itself in darkness the better to avoid chance discovery as it crept stealthily upon its prey.

The whole scene was getting on his nerves! With a deep-chested growl, the burly Karjixian shook himself and cast off his spooky speculations. Probably, the answer to the question was simplicity itself: perhaps

Kan Zar Kan had only observed real human cities by daylight, and had no way of knowing the lengths to which men go to illuminate their centers of population after nightfall.

The citadel was nearer now: he eyed it thoughtfully. If he managed to gain entry unobserved and unmolested, was able to search the towering ziggurat in satisfactorily thorough manner and did not find Ganelon Silvermane, then he had no idea where else to seek his missing friend.

But—first things first. The central structure was the most obvious place to look for the bronze man. He would worry about what to do after that when the time came.

Grrff was completely practical and methodical, and took things as they came.

Suddenly, the whistling silence was broken by the shrill and clamor of alarms. Grrff started, jumped four inches into the air and cursed himself for his jumpiness. Had he accidentally tripped some warning device, unwittingly announcing his presence? Hefting the ygdraxel he had retrieved from the municipal stores, he peered about for some type of robotic guards, monitors or police. He found none.

Then a deep, calm voice spoke out of thin air, echoing through the length of the City.

"Attention all Citizens! This is your City speaking. I am about to suffer attack by unknown enemies who will strike simultaneously from the Earth's surface and the upper atmosphere! All attempts to enter into electronic communication with this unknown foe have proved futile. But fear not, people of Kan Zar Kan! Your City will defend its inhabitants against exterior molestation with the utmost vigor and ingenuity its mentation tanks are capable of! Remain in your homes and be of good cheer: The City has never yet been conquered or even invaded. If all Citizens do their part in our Civil Defense program, we shall elude or destroy our enemies without serious harm. Evasive maneuvers will begin in approximately nine seconds. Secure a comfortable position in a prone posture, if you please, to avoid being flung about and thereby bruising yourselves against my edges. Evasive action begins—*now!*"

And the City took an abrupt curve at right angles to its former course. Grrff was flung off-balance and he cracked his head against the curbing. His skull rang and he saw stars. Shaking his head furiously, he got to his feet and peered around intently to discern the nature of the attack.

From the upper works of the forward traveling edge of the City, lamps cast a piercing actinic glare on the prairie directly ahead. Peering down the length of the street whereon he stood, Grrff saw nothing but an endless plain of waving grasses, formerly cloaked in darkness but not brilliantly illuminated by the stabbing rays.

The night was young and the Falling Moon had not yet entered the sky. By the searchlights, Grrff now saw a turmoil of sudden activity far out on the grassy plains. Thousands of small, scuttling bow-legged figures, vaguely humanoid in appearance, came into view. They seemed to have diverted their course to intercept the Mobile City. They were too small or too distant, or perhaps both, for him to mark them clearly. The City was now moving at such velocity that their small, waddled figures were mere blurs against the brightly-lit field.

Then something fairly large swooped down low over the City and burst like deadly fireworks, becoming a drifting cloud of small red lights. Grrff looked up, shading his eyes against the ruddy glare. The slowly falling red balls of flame exploded with deafening concussions when they came into contact with the upper tiers, tower-tops or aerial walkways. One red fireball struck an empty bubble car and the resultant explosion tore the plastic vehicle asunder. Shards of red hot plastic showered the street and rooftops directly beneath.

The City was indeed under attack. But —by whom?

Staring up into the black sky, Grrff strove to discern the nature of the air assault. Then more searchlights snapped on, spearing the sky, snaring a flying vehicle in their shafts of brilliance.

Now Grrff could see the air enemy clearly—and he roared with astonishment at what he saw.

# 26.

# *IN THE RED ZIGGURAT*

Ganelon stared, grunted with surprise, then relaxed grinning happily. For the person who had addressed him from the darkness of the room proved to be a remarkably handsome young woman in a state of nudity, brandishing a longsword in one small, capable fist. A young woman with tousled red hair, sharp green eyes and a dusting of freckles across the bridge of her small snub nose.

It was Xarda, the girl knight of Jemmerdy!

She was almost as surprised to see him as he was to see her. Her green eyes widened and she started to ask him some inane question like "What are *you* doing here?", when she was suddenly reminded of her state of undress. Dropping her sword (which thumped to the carpet), she snatched a sheet from the bed in which she had been sleeping and hastily held it before her.

"It's not that I am sorry to see you," she grexed, "but, gadzooks, must you come popping through the window of a lady's bedchamber?"

Ganelon solemnly apologized, explaining the situation. Then he released a torrent of questions which the Sirix of Jemmerdy stilled with a lifted palm.

"Save all that for later, can't you? The magister will want to be apprised of your arrival. I'll get dressed now—if you *don't* mind!"

Ganelon loitered in the hallway until she rejoined him a few moments later, now bedecked with odds and ends of steel armor which she thought were decent and proper garb for a young woman. She led him through a maze of rooms into a huge chamber mostly filled with towering banks of machinery where the Illusionist toiled, his silken robes besmirched with daubs of graphite lubricant. He was delighted to see Ganelon, but it was obvious his attentions were elsewhere.

"Thought you'd be turning up before long," he murmured abstractedly. "Wherever have you been all this while? Getting into trouble as usual, I'll hazard! Never mind: tell me later. Must get these switches connected to the power source . . ."

Above them, a huge lens swung about to observe the grouping amiably. A toneless mechanical voice spoke from a grill situated beneath the lens.

"I perceive you have been joined by one of my more recent Citizens," the voice stated calmly.

"Yes," grunted the old magician briefly. "Ganelon, meet the City. City, this is my associate Ganelon, called Silvermane."

Never having been formally introduced to a city before, Ganelon groped for something to say. The City, on the other hand, felt no such restraints.

"How do you do, Ganelon-Called-Silvermane? Welcome to myself. Enjoy your stay here. Should you desire to reside within me permanently, the Immigration Bureau opens tomorrow morning at nine. All applications considered promptly. While you are within me, do not neglect to see the several major tourist attractions. The Red Ziggurat, which is the largest metal building presently extant in Greater Zuavia. The Fire Fountain, newly restored and renovated. An aerial tour via bubble car can be arranged."

"Oh, do be quiet, City!" the magician said, testily. "These connections are tricky." The voice lapsed into silence on the half-syllable.

"How did you get here, anyway?" asked Ganelon of Xarda in low tones. She told him briefly of their escape from Chx and how they had discovered the Bazonga rendered temporarily inoperable, having run into the

Vanishing Mountains head-first; how they had searched Chx and Dwarfland for him and would have extended the quest to include the Land of Red Magic, had not the witless Bird flown them into the northern plains country.

"Well, that's where I was, all right," said Silvermane. While the Illusionist listened with half an ear, swearing under his breath at the wiring problems, the young giant explained how the Death Dwarves had captured him and turned him over to Red Magic legionnaires. He told of his captivity by the Enchantress, his escape with Grrff and Phadia, their weird interdimensional trip through the hyperspatial tube, their stay with the Old Dragon, and so on.

By the time Ganelon had concluded an account of his most recent adventures, the magician had finished rewiring the City's bypass unit, as he explained it to be.

"The City desires nothing more than to become a real city, which implies a stationary locale; but the prime directives implanted in its mentation tanks force it to continually wander about hunting for ore deposits which it no longer has any reason to mine," he explained, wiping his hands on a bit of waste.* "These emergency bypass circuits, which I have just installed, should enable the poor thing to get around those of the directives which it no longer wishes to obey. So you fell into the toils of Zelmarine, heh? Remember how I spirited you out of Zermish to keep you from her clutches? Well, you seem to, ah, have escaped her dominions unscathed: tell me, dear boy, did you find out what it was she wanted you for?"

---

* Ganelon had never before seen the Illusionist's bare hands, or for that matter, any portion of his anatomy unclothed, due to his habitually wearing a mask, robes and gloves. The Epic at this point explains that his hands, while completely human in appearance and structure, were the color of silver. Originally, this meant nothing to me, so I eliminated it from my redaction of the text at this point. But in the light of something mentioned in the Third Book, it does indeed seem significant, hence I have restored it to the text at this point.

Ganelon, with a shamefaced glance at Xarda, blushed darkly crimson.

"Well, uh . . ."

"I see, just as I thought! For breeding purposes. And did you succumb to her wiles in that direction?"

"Well, I, uh . . ."

"Good! The last thing this part of Gondwane needs is a race of immortal supermen fired with ambitions of an imperial destiny. Providing she did not abstract a sample of your sperm for artificial insemination while you slept or were drugged or enchanted, she may still be after you. Red Magic, her specialty you know, works through the human aura. Her abilities to detect individual auric spectra from over a great distance may lead to a further confrontation between us. Let us hope this does not occur."

Ganelon, happy to change the subject, inquired after Erigon and the Bazonga. The Illusionist sniffed.

"Prince Erigon doubtless sleeps in his apartments here in the Red Ziggurat. The City was more than happy to employ its transmutation factories for the production of room furnishings, carpets, bedding and the like, once I explained to it that humans require such luxuries for their comforts. Hence, several apartments here in the Brain Complex have been reserved and furnished for our usage. As for the dear Bird, she is probably cruising about in the central air duct, which is as large as a wind tunnel. It amuses her to improve her flying skills in this manner. Now, m' boy, I am interested in what you say about the Iomagoths. The City is aware of them, of course, and wishes they would come out of the sewers and settle down in any of the houses or cottages already standing. The City will, of course, furnish these according to their wishes. It has promised to equip them with sanitation facilities and running water, now that the poor mechanism understands these human requirements. You must introduce me to the chieftain of the gypsies, so that I may attempt to coax him and his tribe to accept the accomodations the City offers . . . Great Galendil, what's *that?*"

'*That*' was a muffled clangor and shriek—the municipal alarm system, as heard from within the central edifice.

A moment later, the loudspeakers in the Ziggurat came on and made the identical announcement which had so surprised Grrff the Tigerman on the street.

The Illusionist asked the City who or what was attacking it. In response, a large ground-glass screen lit with swirling colors which resolved themselves, by split-screen process, into a three-dimensional view of the forces striking simultaneously from the ground and from the air.

A vista of artificially-lit meadowland swam into focus, filled with stunted, scurrying green imps. Behind them, mounted on prancing white *Ornitho*hippi, came troops of human soldiery in red armor of curious design.

"Death Dwarves, and a back-up regiment of Red Magic soldiers," mused the Illusionist worriedly. "That means . . . my prediction was correct. The Enchantress has traced you here and is making an all-out effort to recapture you!"

The split-screen showed, on its upper half, a fantastic vista of blowing clouds pierced by searchlights. A flying chariot came into view: standing therein, holding the reins in one hand, the Red Queen towered. Her glossy, darkly crimson locks flowing behind her like a tattered banner, the expression on her face was that of a vengeful Fury. The sky chariot was drawn by a matched team of green-scaled, bat-winged, two-legged wyverns.

In her right hand she bore a long iron staff with a flared tip. A spluttering red light blazed in this flared cup. When she gestured, a shower of red fireballs was sprinkled forth on the winds, drifting down to detonate with resounding bangs against the streets and buildings of the Mobile City.

"I am adopting evasive tactics," advised the City,

swerving from its path to avoid the onslaught of the ground forces. But the Red Magic legion was too quick for it, and diverted their own advance to intercept Kan Zar Kan on its new course.

"Stand by for collision," announced the City calmly.

A moment later, the forward edge of the City encountered the vanguard of the Death Dwarves and the Red Magic soldiers. The vision screen tilted its angle of vision to show what occurred at the moment of impact.

And Xarda screamed—!

# 27.

# BATTLE ON THE ENDLESS PLAIN

As the forward edge of the City came into contact with the vanguard of the Death Dwarves and the Red Magic legion, something wonderful and terrible occurred.

The dwarvish little green monsters were suddenly snatched up by an invisible force which bowled them over. Squalling and kicking furiously, they were drawn out of sight under the lip of the vast metal dish on which the City was built.

A moment later, the same irresistible force struck the Red Magic warriors. They were torn out of their saddles, some of them, and flew through the air to vanish beneath the City's edge. Others were drawn beneath the City, *Ornith* and all. It was mysterious and appalling.

The City itself, no longer floating a few yards above the Purple Plain on its air-cushion, now settled towards the meadow's surface. Its undercarriage mechanisms prevented it from sinking down into the grass. Still, the lip of Kan Zar Kan stood ten feet or so above the planetary surface.

The inexplicable force continued to suck in the attacking force, underneath the Mobile City. Now, as the enormous edge of the Moon began to rise up over the horizon, and to augment by its silvery glare the illumination afforded by the City's searchlights, the effects of the mystery force could be more clearly observed. The purple grass itself with literally being

175

pulled out of the soil, tugging and straining at its roots in a frenzied effort to fly into the undercarriage mechanism. It was quite inexplicable.

Inexplicable, that is, to all save the Illusionist. The old magician caught on almost at once. He yowled with glee, hopping from one foot to another in a capering dance. Xarda, Erigon and Silvermane stared at him without comprehension.

"Don't you understand, you simpletons?" the Illusionist crowed. "The air-cushion upon which the City rides is *reversible!* Under normal circumstances, the air is drawn in the side vents by the suction of powerful fans and is thrust out beneath the City, but Kan Zar Kan has simply reversed the circulation of air. Now, it is being sucked in by the powerful fans which normally expel it. That powerful suction is the force which has irresistibly pulled the little green horrors and Zelmarine's soldiers into the mechanism. At any moment, we may expect the City to reverse the system and we shall see the results—*ah, hah!*"

The faint whirring of the air system changed to a full-throated drone. Suddenly the City opened its side vents, spewing forth a gory rain which sprinkled the surrounding meadows with something remarkably like a thin, stocky chowder. The fluid was mixed with lumps, shreds of green dwarf flesh and soldier meat, as well as scraps of white fluff from the unfortunate *Orniths*.

The flesh of the Death Dwarves was tough, and so was the armor of the Red Magic legionnaires. But, quite obviously, not tough enough to avoid being sliced to tiny gobbets when it was drawn through the whirling blades of the fans.

Now the City slid forward some seventy feet, again reversed its air suction, and made further disastrous inroads upon the remainder of Zelmarine's force which broke its lines and attempted to flee in all directions. A full score of Red Magic attackers were sucked into the fans, steed, saddle, soldier and all: a few escaped, spurring their swift-footed bird-horses into flight. As for the remaining Death Dwarves, the bandy-legged little monsters could not run very fast and therefore sought to elude the dreadful suction by burrowing under the meadow. The City remorselessly sucked them squealing and kicking out of their hasty holes, and a few moments later exhaled a ghastly greenish soup in all directions. The Battle of the Purple Plain had been won—on land, at least.

The angle of the vision screen tilted sharply, as the lenses traversed aloft. Evidently, the City was capable of doing two things at once, for now they saw the Enchantress safely imprisoned in a dull glassy sphere against whose durable curvature she raged impotently, hurling small red thunderbolts which only splattered in miniature explosions of sparks against the glassy stuff which encircled her.

"However did you do that?" marveled the old magician delightedly.

"An indestructible plastic of my own manufacture," said the City complacently. "I generally employ it for lining the sewers. It required very little adjustment to extrude it skywards from the spouts, spinning it into a globe."

Some chemical formulae appeared on the screen. The Illusionist studied them briefly, then nodded with satisfaction.

"Splendid stuff! Even the power of Red Magic cannot reduce that form of matter to dust. Well then, congratulations, City! You have won your first battle without the loss of a single life."

Xarda eyed the raging Queen dubiously.

"That's all very well, I'm sure," the girl knight observed cooly. "But it does not really solve the problem, you know."

"Problem? What problem?" sniffed the magician.

The Sirix of Jemmerdy shrugged. "Now that you've got her, what do you intend doing with her?" she inquired practically. "Sending her back to Shai will do no good, you know. By my troth, she's wild with fury: once she gets out of there, she'll be hot on our trail again. Defeat is a mortal insult to her. The poor City will never be safe, so long as she lives."

Prince Erigon swallowed, grimacing fastidiously. The amiable young man found Xarda attractive and interesting, but at times a trifle too blood-thirsty for comfort. "I say, you don't mean to kill a helpless captive, do you?" he inquired anxiously.

"What else?" demanded Xarda, callously. "As we say back home, 'the only good foe is him who's gone to Galendil'."

"I'm afraid I agree with Xarda," said the Illusionist. "The Enchantress must be disposed of. However, that presents us with quite a problem. Being partly a supernatural entity, she would be quite difficult to destroy. Mere physical force would hardly do the trick, I fear. And, being far from my magical laboratory, I lack at present the magical, ah, 'clout', to work the thing."

They stared at one another thoughtfully. How do you permanently dispose of a dangerous and vindictive enemy who is a bit too powerful to be easily destroyed?

To the surprise of them all, it was Ganelon Silvermane who came up with the best idea. Because the giant youth was rather stolid and slow-speaking, they were all accustomed to thinking of him as being just a bit slower mentally than they were themselves. This, as the Illusionist could have told them, was a fundamental error. Silvermane was possessed of a first-rate brain, but he tended to rely on others to come up with ideas, either out of habitual diffidence or modesty.

"The hyperspatial tube," he said suddenly.

They stared at him uncomprehendingly.

"Eh, my boy, what was that?" asked the Illusionist absently. Silvermane repeated the phrase. They ogled him blankly, so he elaborated on his suggestion.

"The hyperspatial tube. You know, the interdimensional Labyrinth by which Grrff, Phadia and I (of course you haven't met them yet because they're still down in the sewers with all those Iomagoths) escaped from Shai. Once you're inside it, it's awfully hard to figure out where you want to go and just how to get there. Couldn't the City render the plastic sphere opaque, go back to that place on the Plains where we came out, and pop her inside the thing at such a speed that by the time she slowed down and managed to get out of the globe, she'd be thoroughly lost. It might take her years to find her way back to Gondwane again?"

They mulled that over in silence for a time. Then the Illusionist cleared his throat.

"*Ahem!* While your syntax may leave something to be desired in terms of clarity, m'boy, your idea is perfectly feasible. In fact, I can't think of a better solution to our problem myself! I say, City, can you locate the nearest terminus of the Cavern of a Thousand Perils?"

The City, in its pleasantly neutral voice, said that it certainly could. Extruding plastic nets wherein to snare the durable bubble which enclosed the raging but helpless Enchantress, it chased away her wyvern-chariot, which flew off in the general direction taken by the few surviving Red Magic legionnaires. Then, returning to normal traveling circuits, it lifted itself up onto its air cushion and went whiffling off over the blood-bedewed meadow grass in the direction of the terminus, which happened to be due southwest.

Well before morning paled in the east, the Enchantress had been hurled through the interdimensional gate at such extreme velocity that by the time she slowed and came to rest, she should be hopelessly lost somewhere between the worlds, planes, lands and ages connected by the hyperspatial network.

Doubtless, she would never be able to bother any of them again. Or so they hoped, anyway. Privately, the Illusionist was not so sure. But time would tell, as always.

# 28.

# THE CITY MOVES NORTH

Ganelon came out of the Red Ziggurat about the same time as Grrff succeeded in entering it. The burly Karjixian was delighted and relieved to see his friend safe and whole, but was mighty mystified by all the recent goings-on.

"Ho, big man! Still in one piece, eh? Grrff is happy to find you at last," rumbled the Tigerman. "But whatever has been happening in this cursed walking city, anyway? First Drng's little green devils attack, then—*whoosh!*—they go splattering all over the plain in bite-size chunks; then the Red Bitch is somehow globed up and the crazy city goes zipping back south again—"

Ganelon explained as best he could what was behind the recent events, then introduced the affable Grrff to his friends, Erigon, Xarda and the Illusionist. About that same time the Bazonga, considerably ruffled and besplattered, emerged from the ducts to indignantly inquire about who had turned on the garbage. While she was being mollified and cleaned up a bit, Yemple and his cohorts emerged timidly from the nearer sewer-grille, quite shaken up by the recent inexplicable happenings. Introductions were made all around and the entire population of Kan Zar Kan gathered timidly in a nearby square for an impromptu picnic breakfast while the Illusionist harangued the cowed, bewildered Iomagoths and formally introduced them to their host.*

---

* That is, to the City itself.

"Kan Zar Kan is a changed City," he told them. "It wishes for nothing more than to become your friendly and cooperative home on a permanent basis. It now understands about 'too much cleaning-up' and furnishings and such-like. Already, the robot factories are turning out cushions, carpets, window-curtains and kitchenware. If you will promise to settle here without attempting to escape, the City will consider all pleas, petitions and other requests from your elective spokesmen. Quite frankly, it is anxious to please. The City yearns to settle down in one place permanently and enter into trade with nearby civilizations. It remains armed and alert to defend its inhabitants against all foes. Well, what do you Iomagoths say?"

King Yemple hemmed and hawed, raised quibbles and questions; but the womenfolk were ogling the array of new home furnishings temptingly displayed in the shopwindows, which had a direct conduit to the robot factories. The last vestige of Iomagothic reluctance vanished when Yemple learned that the most imposing edifice of the City—the Red Ziggurat itself—would of course be reserved as the residence of the royal family. Articles of Mutual Agreement were drawn up on the instant, with Ganelon and the Illusionist as chief witnesses to the signing.

After breakfast, the Iomagoths went on a guided tour of their beautiful new kingdom by bubble cars, which were now subservient to the wishes of their riders, while our friends considered their next course of action. Now that Zelmarine was more or less permanently out of the picture, the Illusionist was eager to reconnoiter the third of the major menaces he foresaw as threatening the peace and security of Northern YamaYamaLand.* Prince Erigon was more than pleased at this news, for the third menace was none other than the restive and warlike Ximchak Horde, currently threatening his own country of Valardus. The

---

* The first threat, already disposed of, was that of the Airmasters of Sky Island, and the second was the Red Enchantress herself.

mild-mannered, rather soft-spoken young Prince was putting his head together with the Illusionist over plans when an unexpected visitation shattered the peaceful calm of the square.

As a scarlet, lobster-like ghoul-monster with many pincers and twice as many eyes suddenly materialized out of thin air amongst the picnic things, the Prince turned white as salt, jumped three feet into the air and uttered an anguished yelp. When he came down, he was off and running for the nearest sewer: only the Bazonga was fast enough to intercept him in his flight. She snared him by closing her bronze beak on the skirt of his tunic, giving him a playful nip in the process.

"Tuth! Idth on'y Fridth," she chided, mumblingly.

"What did you say?"

Releasing him, she cleared her throat. "Hard to talk with your mouth full, you know, Princey-dear! I said, 'Tush! It's only Fryx'."

"Did you say *only?*" shrilled the Prince incredulously. "It's a Gyraphont, that's what it is! I know a Gyraphont when I see one, I do! My nurse used to frighten me half to death with them when I had been, well, unruly. 'The Gyraphonts come to get bad little boys in the night,' she would say, the old horror! *Only* a Gyraphont, indeed!"

"Oh, come on Prince, stop acting the milksop," sneered Xarda, swaggering over to where the Valardan stood, his bony knees clattering together like wooden castanets. "Fryx is the magister's pet Gyraphont, quite tame and perfectly harmless." Somewhat reluctantly, Erigon allowed himself to be coaxed back to where the scarlet lobster-devil stood conversing telepathically with the old magician.

*You come back home now, holay?* the weird monstrosity urged. *No more zip-zoop around all over? Flion, he moultin' and won't eat, vat-critters all off they feed, an' Vloob Atz allatime pickin 'fights with tin man. Lotsa mail pilin' up, too.*

Frowning worriedly behind his vapory vizor, the Illusionist turned to Erigon as he cautiously approached.

"I fear we shall have to postpone our plans to reconnoiter the situation in Valardus, my dear Prince," he said. "My faithful Fryx informs me I am urgently needed at home. The creatures in my private menagerie of fabulous monsters are missing me to the point of malnutrition, and my pet apparition is indulging his vile temper in spats with Azgelazgus, one of my favorite Automatons."

"That's too bad," murmured Erigon faintly, eyeing the scarlet, many-armed lobster-ghoul dubiously.

"It's my own fault. I have been away from Nerelon far too long. Fryx has coped admirably thus far, but I fear I can no longer postpone a brief visit to put things right at my residence. Enchanted palaces are tricksey places under the best of conditions, you know. At times they need a firm hand on the reins, so to speak."

"Quite all right, I'm sure," said Erigon.

"Does that mean the expedition to the north country is canceled?" inquired Silvermane. The old magician shook his head.

"Merely postponed, my boy, for a brief while."

"Well, what about our plans for taking Xarda home? Back to Jemmerdy, I mean."

"By my troth, Jemmerdy can wait," the girl knight said spiritedly. "Our new-found comrade hath a cause, the which appeals to mine sense of Chivalry! Let us free the noble folk of sieged Valardus from the savage rabble first, ere any think of going home."

They eyed her a bit askance. The Sirix flushed, biting her lip vexedly. She had more-or-less fallen out of her native mode of speech in their rough-and-ready company. From time to time, however, the antique mode came over her, as now.

She cleared her throat, leveling a defiant glare at any who might think to venture upon a chuckle. With none forthcoming, the girl knight relaxed and grinned a bit sheepishly.

"No, all kidding aside, really! I mean, look, why don't you go on back home, magister. The rest of us can continue on to Valardus and await you there," suggested Xarda, practical-minded as ever.

"I shall be taking the Bazonga bird," said the Illusionist, "which would be leaving you with no method of transportation except for shank's-mare. 'Twould hardly be fair, asking you to cross the Purple Plains on foot—"

"What about the kayak?" piped up Phadia, who had been listening to this exchange with a crestfallen look on his pretty face, sorry that their adventures were at an end.

"You're right, of course," said the magician, surprised. "Istrobian's flying kayak! Why, I had forgotten all about it!"

"I tied it to a stanchion back in the air duct," said the Bazonga carelessly. "It interfered with my flying-practice, having that great lumbering thing tied to my tail-feathers."

"Hmm, the kayak only seats four, you know. Ganelon, Xarda, Erigon, Grrff, Phadia. One of you will have to return to Nerelon with me, or walk. I suspect it should be *you,* my lad," he said, with a fond glance at the young boy.

"But, sir, I want to have some more adventures!" protested Phadia, tears starting in his eyes.

"You've had quite enough adventures as it is," said the magister with mock-severity. "Time you had a good hot bath, some real home cooking, and a few lessons in reading, writing, arithmetic, and razzledoxy!"

"But—!" Phadia screwed up his face and was about to burst into a storm of girlish sobs when Grrff enfolded him in a comforting, furry arm.

"Posh and pother, cub! Go along with the nice old human, now—you can join us, later on!" Xarda chimed in with some heartening words, and Ganelon solemnly began describing the many marvels of the Illusionist's mountaintop abode, not neglecting to list the scrumptious, succulent meals Fryx was always shoving before them. Before long the lad was eagerly contemplating his chance to visit the enchanted palace of a world-famous magician, an opportunity few boys his age could hope to enjoy.

And then the City itself spoke up, offering to take the four northwards to Valardus using its mobility as means of transport. One last jaunt, before it settled down to becoming a regular City that stayed in one place all the time, seemed only fitting and proper.

"A delightful notion, my dear City," nodded the magician. "And should you find Valardus occupied by the Ximchak barbarians, simply remember to reverse your suction as you did with the Death Dwarves! Capital, capital! Why, I may rejoin you to find half the Horde already chopped into minced meat!"

The farewells were brief, though heart-felt. Ganelon had never been separated from his master for any length of time since he had left home nearly a year ago, but he was consoled by the fact that the separation was to be only a temporary thing. The Illusionist bundled the eager-faced Phadia into the Bazonga. Before the noontide sun had quite ascended to its zenith, the ungainly flying contraption rose, circled the plaza clacking her excited goodbys, and flew off to the southwest, dwindling to a tiny mote in the distance. Fryx, of course, had taken his usual interdimensional shortcut and would be home before them, doubtless in time to have a fire lit in the great pillared hall, hot baths drawn, and huge mugs of steaming chocolate ready with heaping platters of sandwiches and cookies.

Ganelon stood gazing after the Bazonga, feeling empty, forlorn and somehow deserted. But before long the City started upward and began flying across the interminable meadows north, towards Valardus and an exciting host of new adventures among strange foreign lands and curious peoples.

It is hard to remain melancholy when faced with such an entertaining prospect. Shrugging off his solemn mood, Ganelon Silvermane turned on his heel and went over to where his friends were already getting set to have lunch with the happy, chattering band of Iomagoths.

Gliding steadily on, north and ever north, Kan Zar Kan itself gradually dwindled and shrank until at last it vanished, lost in the distance. What perils and adventures lay ahead for the little band of heroes, only time would tell.

## THE END.

# APPENDIX

## A GLOSSARY OF UNFAMILIAR NAMES AND TERMS

*Chx:*

The small city-state of Chx, together with its neighboring realms of Ning, Quay, Horx, Poy, Cham, and possibly Ixland (for some students of Gondwanology consider the original name of that country to have been "Ik"), are the remnants of the Monosyllabic Empire which flourished in these border regions of Northern YamaYamaLand in the early millennia of the present Eon. After the collapse and breakup of Monosyllabia, former provinces or counties achieved their independence and embarked on the troubled path of self-rule. Old customs died hard during this period, while personal and tribal names gradually developed into polysyllabism. Place-names, more securely rooted in ancient tradition, remained words of one syllable. Chelibus has an interesting monograph on this subject.

*Dianium:*

According to leading authorities on Alchemy, a metal found only on the Moon, whose strongest urge is to return to its satellitic home. One of the living, or at least sentient metals, such as *glegium.* (for which see pertinent data in the Third Book of the Epic, forthcoming). Technically, *dianium* is element 122 on the Periodic Table, and the known isotope of *dianium* with the longest halflife has an atomic weight of 273. The sentient or Living Metals are considered of recent origin, cosmically speaking; only with publication of Cardoxicus' milestone theorem, *The Evolution of the Elements,* was it realized that the doctrine of evolution could be extended to matter itself, and that all things in the Plenum tend towards vitality, if not indeed intelligence.

### Greater Zuavia:

The land-surface of Gondwane was so vast by the time of Ganelon Silvermane that it had long-since become impractical for historians or geographers to discuss individual countries as such. A new geo-historical term, which I translate as "conglomerate," has been coined in order to deal with groups of countries as entities. Such conglomerates were composed of several individual realms which were individually autonomous, but linked together by a common ethnic origin or by common adherence to a religious creed. Southern and Northern Yama-YamaLand were two such conglomerates: the twin conglomerates were originally settled by the Yamiac Nomads, a migrant horde of *yax*-herders who strayed into these grassy regions one million years before. They were forced to invent or adopt urban civilization when the *yax* herds succumbed *en-masse* to the Giggling Fever. Originally divided into East YamaLand and West YamaLand, the northern countries became united during a wholesale conversion to the Zul-and-Rashemba Mythos and were simply known as "YamaYamaLand." The southern half of the race remained true to the parent creed of the Mythos, which was Old High Great Quaxianity, hence the division into north and south.

As for Zuavia, which lies beyond the Purple Plains to the north, the Plains forming a natural border between the conglomerates, both Greater

Zuavia and its sister-conglomerate to the east, Lesser Zuavia, were established some two and a half million years ago. The Zuaves wandered down from their mythic homeland on the shores of Zuav, the Sacred River. Originally, they were descended from a forgotten race called the Paniche. Greater Zuavia, the scene of the Third and Fourth Books of the Epic, comprises some twenty-two separate realms. They are purely Zuavic in ethnos and religiously devoted to the several creeds of the Peshtite Mysterium. Greater Zuavia is half again the size of Europe.

*Istrobian:*

Towards the middle of the "current" Eon—current in context of the Epic, that is—flourished a brief period known as the Age of Magicians, or more formally, the Epoch of the High Wizards. Human civilization was for the most part dominated by the rise to power of some ninety major magicians. This period had long since lapsed by the time of our story, but the effects of this minor Age of Magicians still reverberated in human affairs. Among the High Wizards of the epoch were several who have some bearing on our story, such as the celebrated Clesper Volphotex to whom Grrff refers in Chapter 10 of the present book, the famous Miomivir Chastovix who is mentioned several times in the First Book; the notorious Palensus Choy who appears in the Third; and Istrobian, a distinguished sorcerer of Greater Zuavia. The flying kayak was only one of his many celebrated achievements, among which were the Star Lens, Istrobian's Fire-Flasher, the Earth Tube and the Submarine City. Many consider this last to be purely legendary, however. Oddly enough, the Illusionist of Nerelon does not seem to be a survivor of this Epoch, despite his evidently considerable longevity which should have made him a contemporary of these celebrities. The author of the Ninth Commentary postulates that the Illusionist was extant during the Age of the Magicians, but maintained a low profile for some peculiar reason. The question is still unresolved.

## Magic:

Some sixty of the Secret Sciences were known and practiced in Ganelon's day, more than half of which fall into the category of the Divinatory Arts, such as seership, astromancy, fortune-telling, Greater, Lesser and Middle Prophecy, haruspexy and theomancy. Three others were among the Alchemic or Metamorphosical Sciences. As for magic *per se,* which may be defined as employment of various world forces to alter, affect or manipulate Reality, twenty of these were studied during this period. Among these were Red Magic, which employs the Auric force from whose sanguinary coloration (to the Astral vision, at least) the name is derived; Green Magic, which taps the earth current itself; Purple Magic, and also Mountain Magic, which are among the several forms of Elemental Goety, and which utilize the Gnomic elemental force; Air Magic, and its variant, Blue Magic, which use the Sylphic force according to different modes; White Magic, which taps the Celestial force; Black Magic, which employs the Demonic or Infernal; and Gray Magic, which taps the Halfworld current. Sea Magic, Metal Magic, Star Magic and Yellow Magic were virtually in their infancy during this period, and did not flower until the following Eon. Fire Magic, another of the Elemental variety, employs the Salamandric force. Beyond these, and the others I have too little space to describe or even list, there were the four arts of Thaumaturgy *per se;* that is, the Astral, the Vitalic, the Psychonic and the Phonemic, and one other magical science unpracticed by humans or Quasi-humans, but known to them and reserved for the Gods only.

The only practitioner of Phonemic Thaumaturgy

mentioned in the entire Epic is Zelobion of Karchoy, who appears in the Eighth Book; from this, the Commentaries deduct the art was either one of extreme rarity or extreme newness, or both.

### Red Amazons, the:

An all-but-extinct race of quasi-humans who formerly inhabited the islands of the Cham Archipelago near Thoph, in the remote southwestern corner of the Supercontinent. Although evolved from True Human stock (or such as was the prevailing opinion of the period), the Amazons were considerably larger, stronger, more intelligent, durable and longer-lived than the other human or human-derived races of the Eon. The reason why such Superwomen died out remains an enigma, although the author of the Sixteenth Commentary (notedly, if not indeed notoriously, pious), attributes their extinction to a direct act of intervention into human affairs by the god Galendil himself.

The Cham Archipelago, by the way, has no known connection with the Cham Empire directly north of Shai beyond the Mountains of the Death Dwarves, extending as far as the southern shore of the Glass Sea. It is unfortunately obliterated on my map in this book by the legend. Since there were one hundred and thirty-seven thousand individual countries in Gondwane during this period, and since the Gondwanish language only consists of twenty-nine phonemes, capable of assembly into a strictly finite number of combinations, many hundreds of place-names were duplicated by sheer inadvertence.

### Tigermen of Kàrjixia, the:

A fairly civilized race of Nonhumans evolved from a chance mutation to sentience in *Panthera tigris*, some fifty thousand years before the period of Ganelon Silvermane. This, at least, is the currently popular opinion. According to the Savants of Nembosch, the mutation was implemented by the notorious supermagician, Palensus Choy, the so-called "Immortal of Zaradon," whom we will encounter in the Third Book.

*Ygdraxel:*

Traditional weapon habitually employed by the Tigermen of Karjixia in war; a sort of tridentiform billhook terminating in long, razory, collapsible hooks. Obviously, the Tigermanic weapon, unique to the armory of Karjixia, was a mechanical elaboration on the design of a cat's claws.


End Of The Glossary